1
Rode a Horse of Milk White Jade

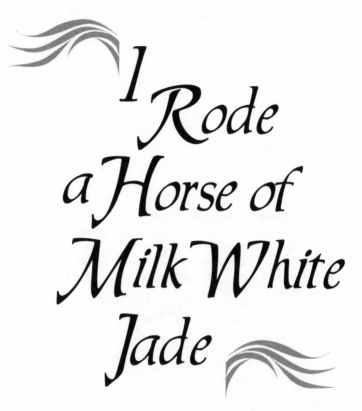

I Rode a Horse of Milk White Jade

DIANE LEE WILSON

Orchard Books • New York

Dedicated to my dear friend Florence Caldwell,
who shared her love for horses and
started me on my own journey.

Orchard Books, 95 Madison Avenue, New York, NY 10016

Manufactured in the United States of America
Book design by Mina Greenstein
Map by Susan Detrich
The text of this book is set in 12 point Imprint.
10   9   8   7   6   5   4   3   2   1

Library of Congress Cataloging-in-Publication Data
Wilson, Diane L.
I rode a horse of milk white jade / by Diane L. Wilson.
p.   cm.
Summary: Oyuna tells her granddaughter the story of how love
for her horse enabled her to win a race and bring good luck
to her family living in Mongolia in 1285.
ISBN 0-531-30024-2 (trade : alk. paper). —
ISBN 0-531-33024-9 (lib. bdg. : alk. paper)
[1. Horses—Fiction. 2. Mongolia—Fiction. 3. Luck—Fiction.]
I. Title.
PZ7.W69057Iae   1998   [Fic]—dc21   97-23838

CONTENTS

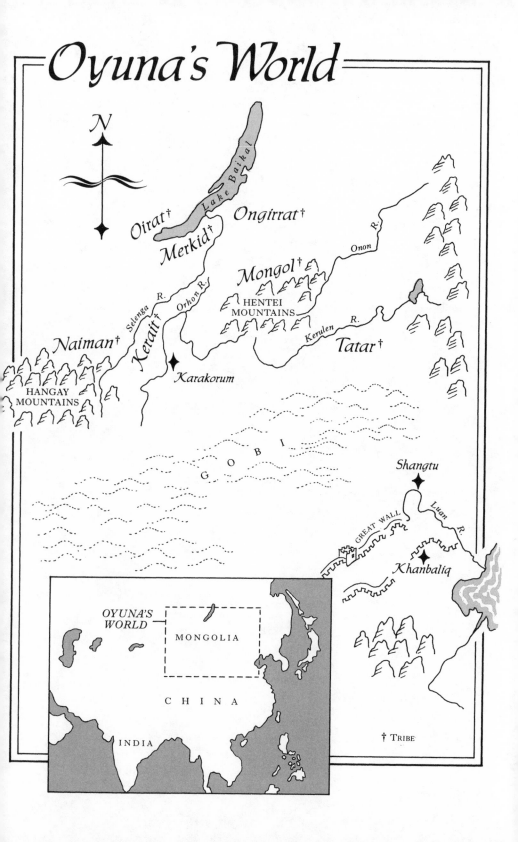

Outside Hangchou, China— A.D. 1339

"Grandmother! You came!"

"Of course I came."

"But it's so far, and with your leg being—"

"Never you mind what can't be changed. How is she?"

"I don't know. Not well, I think. She's just been circling all day."

"Circling." The wrinkled face nodded. Papery eyelids drooped, then lifted on dove gray eyes flecked with gold. "That is good. Circling brings luck. Circling . . . completes the journey."

Head bobbing, the heavily robed old woman lifted the latch and limped into the stable's shadows. She pulled the shivering girl into the sweet-smelling grass piled in the corner. Together they silently marveled at the swollen sides of the white mare who stood, ears pricked, staring expectantly into the night.

"See?" A knobby finger was thrust from beneath the

fraying edge of the deep blue silk robe. "She knows to wait for the right time. We will wait with her." Opening her robe and pulling the young girl within its warmth, the old woman continued, "Your mother tells me you have many questions—about what happened in the past." A sigh, like a weak breeze sifting through dried leaves, floated into the darkness. "That was long ago, a different time, a different land even. But perhaps, before the night is through . . ."

The white ears of the mare flickered forward and back, trying to catch the low tones drifting through her stall. But the woman whispered her story only for her granddaughter, whose small body curled beneath her arm. It was the ninth day of the ninth month; the moon rose full. The time had come.

1. The Black Mare

I don't remember on which day it happpened. I do remember the earth warm against my back, the dirt soft beneath my fingernails as I cried out. So it must have been June, or maybe July, for the months of summer are but fleeting visitors in Mongolia.

Before the hands came, pulling me up, before the voice joined mine, wailing, in that brief moment of chaos where all becomes calm, there was the mare. As I lay upon my back, a helpless, whining toddler, she lowered her head to nuzzle me. Like the falling of night her great dark head pushed away the pale sky, for she was all I could see. Warm gusts from her giant nostrils blew across my face. Silky black hide, stretched over bony sun and shadow, framed liquid eyes. I stared into their depths. Like black water on a moonless night, they hid what lay beneath, yet drew me in, breathless. I think that in that moment I did hold my breath, stopped crying.

Then the mare lifted her hoof, passing it over my head,

and moved on. She picked her way daintily now, as if fearful of crushing a flower. But there it was already— my crushed foot.

With the rushing pain came the blood; with the blood, the screams. I remember my mother hurriedly wrapping my foot in a silk sash of pale blue—the color of good luck. The blood seeped through anyway, warm and wet, and I could smell it. It is the same smell as when a baby goat plunges into your hands from its mother's womb. The smell of birth.

This was my birth into the realm of the horse.

2. Twilight Is a Magical Time

*O*yuna! Come away from the door flap!''

I heard the worry in my mother's voice, but the horses were galloping along the horizon and my eyes followed where my feet could not. I felt her tugging at my *del*, trying to pull her stubborn seven-year-old daughter, the one who had shaken loose her braid, letting the hair fall in a long black mane, back inside the *ger*.

"Here," she ordered, pressing my fingers one by one around a long wooden spoon. "You stir the soup."

As the newborn baby is wrapped around and around, each felt layer hugging him away from the winds, protecting him, so my family had wrapped me away from a keen-scented world whose laughter I could only hear. Because my foot now dragged clumsily, like a chunk of meat roped to my flopping ankle, I was wrapped inside the thick felt walls of our *ger*. And told to stay.

The filtered glow of each morning's sun found me limping fitfully behind my mother, confined to learning the skills of the hands. Only in the rare moment was I allowed, blinking, into the bold sunshine: to lug water from a stream, to quickly squeeze milk from a goat, or to set fat slices of *aaruul* to dry on our slanting roof. Every day was like the one before it and the one after it.

Stirring. Always there was a pot in the fire to stir: mutton boiling, yogurt thickening, tea leaves brewing. I was still but a child then, sitting lopsided by the fire, clutching the wooden spoon in my small hand, yet I remember feeling—no, I remember knowing, even then—that I was misplaced. *You belong with the horses,* my mind whispered. My eager heart could only whicker a soft response.

When my fingers weren't wrapping a spoon they were pinching a needle. I was taught to mend the tears in the silk *dels* of my mother and father, but as my stitches grew straighter, other members of my *ail* began leaving me their torn clothing. "Too busy," they would say, smiling. I could do it. The gods had at least blessed me with skillful hands. Sometimes I wondered if the sadness I stitched into a *del* followed its wearer, like a shadow, out across the steppes.

And of course there was the beating. For hours each day, until my shoulders ached, I banged a big stick within the bulging sides of the goatskin bag holding *ayrag.* Day after day I pushed that stick through the foamy mare's milk, waiting for it to ferment into the drink so enjoyed by my father and his brothers. The most stifling of tasks, until I discovered that the sloshing echo could be coaxed into hoofbeats: *Thud. Sl-slosh. Thud. Sl-slosh. Thud. Sl-slosh.*

The cadence reawakened my heart, sent it bucking. So much that at nightfall, when my father poked his head through the door flap, I threw myself at him. Rubbed my face against the sleeve of his brown silk *del,* sucked in the sweet, sweaty smell of the horse. And begged to go with him.

"Carry me in the saddle with you," I cried.

Always his stubby fingers tousled my black hair. "No, Oyuna," he would answer, shaking his head. "You are our only child—too precious to let bad luck find you again. Better you stay inside. You are not made to ride."

He tried to fasten his words on me like hobbles. But I, too, shook my head: No! And later, frowning at my twisted foot, I wondered what my parents saw that I didn't. While I was always thinking about horses and what I wanted to do, my mother and father, it seemed, were always thinking about my leg and what I couldn't do. "Bad luck," I heard them whisper to each other. They blew their words into the fire and silently watched the smoke rise, with their prayers, out of the *ger.*

For many years after "that time," as my mother called it, a stuffed-felt doll dressed in the bloody silk sash that had once wrapped my crushed foot sat propped upon the painted wood chest in our *ger.* One foot was dyed red. Oh, how I hated that doll!

Before each meal, before any one of us was allowed to lift food to our lips, an offering of food and drink was first smeared on her staring face. My mother and father made prayers to the doll with the red leg that my own leg might suddenly grow right. Over the years the doll's face grew dark, stained and smelly with food, yet my leg remained crooked.

Every moon or so, our *ail* moved to fresh grazing and then we often crossed the paths of other clans. I learned to cringe at the sight of oxcarts marching along the horizon. For that meant that yet another drum-beating, white-robed shaman would examine my foot. Again prayers were offered, incantations sung, ointments that stank and burned rubbed into my flesh. And sacrifices made. It wasn't until I was older that I learned that the black mare that had stepped on my foot had, at the command of a shaman, been killed. It was her blood that had dyed the foot of the felt doll. The day I learned that, I couldn't eat. Kneeling at dinner across from the dirty-faced doll with the bloody foot, I felt the food stick in my throat.

At one of these meetings of clans I remember noticing a certain boy sitting proudly upon a prancing brown horse. Around the horse's neck was tied a shiny scarf of sky blue silk. I tugged at my mother's sleeve and pointed.

"That boy won the long race at the festival," she explained, bending to whisper in my ear. "His mother says he and that brown gelding of his galloped faster than a hundred others. And so he carries the winner's scarf—and great luck—to both his family and his clan."

She straightened. And as I watched my mother watch the boy's mother stroke the horse's brown neck and clap her son upon the back, how I wanted to press that proud smile onto my own mother's face. But, dropping my gaze to the twisted foot wrapped in its felt boot, I could feel only shame. Wrinkling my nose, I stuck out my tongue.

That night, and for many days and nights afterward, I humbly cringed beneath the leer of the red-footed doll. I began to believe in my parents' prayers. The gods had certainly stamped bad luck upon me. Such was to be my place in this world then: always to huddle within the smoky half-light of a *ger,* only to watch as others galloped upon the backs of swift horses, to startle and quiver at every passing cloud. My childhood seemed defined by what I could not do.

Then one day, just at dusk, I discovered what I could do. Limping through the grasses to fill a bag with water, I came upon a spotted gelding drinking at the stream. Holding my breath, I looked over my shoulder—and saw that all heads were buried in their work, hurrying to finish before dark.

At that shadowy instant I felt as if the horse and I were the only creatures in a far-off place, in a land where all was possible. I just had to try! And at that twilight moment all was possible.

Gently I laid the pouch in the dirt. I spoke to the gelding and he raised his head, ears pricked toward me, water dripping from his lips. Slowly I limped toward him. Placing my hands around his moss-soft muzzle, I blew into his nostrils. He exhaled his warm breath into my face. I ran my hands along his brow, under his thick mane, and down his withers. Then my left hand closed on a hank of mane. Leaning into the warm body, I bounced—once, twice—pushing against the hard earth and finally pulling my crippled leg over his back. Free.

Happiness rose within me, blossoming into a wide grin. At last I was where I belonged.

3. A Discovery, a Decision

*N*o hobbles could hold me then. At every turn of my mother's head I sneaked away from my chores to pull myself onto the back of a horse and race across the steppes. Loud whoops of joy scattered behind us, mingling with the echoing hoofbeats.

My father sighed. My mother fretted. But finally they pulled aside the door flap to our *ger* and released me to the outside world. My mother still worried that my "bad luck" would somehow find me again, so she placed around my neck a braided leather thong on which dangled a small horse of misty green jade. She said it had been given to her by her mother, a shamaness, and held powers to keep me safe. Only then did she agree to teach me the tasks of the outdoors: gathering dung, combing the sheep, helping deliver the animal young. I worked hard, truly I did, yet always my heart thundered with the horses. I was not afraid of bad luck then, for even if it waited along the steppes, I would gallop on by.

One day, in my twelfth spring, my father traded for some barley flour, which was highly prized. My mother and I were inside our *ger,* kneading the dough, and through the smoke hole I could see the blue sky dangling like a brilliant jewel just out of reach. I was supposed to be helping shape the dough into small rounds for frying. But to kneel in the shadows on a day when the winds whispered of secrets just over the next rise, well . . .

"Oyuna!" My mother's voice was scolding but, when I looked up, I saw her brown eyes twinkled. "Barley cakes are supposed to be round, like this. Yours look more like"—squinting, she cocked her head—"like horse hooves! Now, tell me, what will your father say when we serve him horse hoof cakes tonight?" Her tinkling laugh burst forth with mine, for we both could picture my father slapping his hands to his forehead, exclaiming to the gods that they had mistakenly given him a horse in place of a daughter.

In a sweeping motion my mother's arm gathered toward her the lumpy attempts at fetlocks and pasterns. Tongue flitting between her teeth, tsk-tsking noisily, she jerked her head in a direction over my shoulder. "Take the basket, then, and gather some dung for the cooking fire. And don't be a tortoise. Rain comes." With a joyous shriek I hugged my mother's waist and bolted outside.

The afternoon sun glinted in my eyes as I bent to retrieve the large basket used for gathering dung. Tengri, the blue sky spirit, was pleased, for soft puffs of wind fingered my black hair, lifting the plaited ends. Heart beating happily, I balanced the basket across my back like a saddle, clutching the wide leather strap to my chest. Then, whinnying softly, I bent to my task, an honest horse, though a lame one. I knew that had I actually been a horse, my role would have been as dinner for the dogs rather than as worker for the clan. With my long silk *del*—the tawny color of a sandgrouse's underfeathers—rustling against my trousers and stirring a spicy fragrance from the purple and red flowers shivering in the breeze, I gratefully hobbled toward the low rise where the horses had spent the day grazing.

Already this season promised to be my happiest—for at last I fit in. Looking down at my fingers wrapped around the leather chest strap, I saw past the stained nails and cracked skin. I saw hands that knew how to coax a wet and trembling lamb from a birthing ewe, hands that knew how to comb the soft underbelly of a goat without pulling the skin and how to ease between a nursing foal and its protective dam long enough to squeeze a little of the mare's milk into a leather bag. I had shaken off my bad luck, I thought proudly. The shaman came no more. Even my relatives let me work among them without pointing.

My breath was coming hard now with the climb, so I stopped to rest, turning around to gauge my progress. The five round white *gers* of my *ail,* each door facing the south for luck, sat clustered in the valley below me. Already long green shadows stretched protectively across them. In another direction grazed our herd of sheep, like little round clouds dotting the earth, and beyond them I could see that my uncles were rounding up the goats for the evening milking.

Crouching like a predator just above the horizon was a long band of blue-black clouds and I knew that I must gather the dung quickly or there would be little fire within our *ger* that night.

Hobbling up the rise, the basket swaying upon my back, I must have resembled a small camel. Yet in my mind I

was a horse, halting at the crest to sniff the air for danger—
an angry boar whose yellowed tusks could rip through the
belly of a fallen animal, or a hungry long-fanged wolf,
roaming the grasslands for an easy dinner. Turning my
head from side to side, I strained to catch the low growl
of a leopard squatting, tail swishing, in wait. But only a
plaintive mewing met my ears.

"Bator!" I exclaimed as the tiny tiger-striped kitten
bounded into sight, instantly weaving a pattern around
my legs. "What are you doing all the way out here?"

In response Bator jumped onto my padded silk trousers,
needle-sharp claws snagging a path upward. I had found
the kitten two moons ago, dragging his half-starved body
behind one of the oxcarts, and named him Bator, meaning
"hero." Now, I know the giving of a name to an animal
is unheard of, but somehow, to me anyway, Bator seemed
more than a mere animal. He strutted cockily, meowing
loudly, always announcing his accomplishments to the
world. That day, although he was climbing my clothing
with all the courage and determination of his name, I
scooped him up in my hand, cuddling his furry body
beneath my chin. Then I held him out in front of my
face.

"What is it you want, little one?" Again the tiny creature
wailed, his green eyes shutting tight with the effort.

"Oh, is that it? Well, I can't play right now, I have
work to do. And besides, it's going to rain, so we have to
hurry." With great effort Bator stretched a front leg, the
little toes at the end spreading to reveal five tiny pink
pads. He mewed loudly. I chuckled. "I'll bet your feet
are tired after that long walk. How about if you ride in
the basket until I'm done?" Carefully I dropped him into
the basket on my back, but before I could take another

step, Bator had leaped onto my shoulder, mewing urgently in my ear.

"Well, I don't know what you want, you little nuisance, but if you don't want a ride you can walk." I set the squirming animal on the ground. Without looking back, Bator charged through the tall grasses, still crying out.

And then I did know. From the time that kitten had come under my care he had been able, somehow, to make me understand what he wanted. And now he was making me understand that something was wrong and that I needed to follow him. Eyeing the blackness flooding the horizon, I turned to follow.

I could barely see Bator's stubby tail wending its way through the grasses, but his loud mewing served as an effective guide. Ahead, I knew, lay a dried creek bed, strewn with rocks. Bator's cries halted at its edge. Struggling up behind the kitten, I saw the reason for his worry. In the crusty, web-patterned dirt at the bottom lay one of our *ail*'s goats. Her sides were swollen with a late pregnancy and one miniature black foot attached to a spindly black leg protruded from beneath her tail. When she saw me the goat lifted her head and bleated pitifully. Her cry was drowned by the first rumbling of thunder. Helpless, the goat dropped her head back to the hard ground and lay panting, her pink tongue bright against her gaping mouth.

"Oyuna! Come now!" The faint voice of my mother rushed across the steppe on the rising wind. But the storm chased hard behind it. Fat drops of rain began to pelt the three of us.

Wheeling around, I stumbled, a sharp pain darting through my foot as a blast of cold rain struck me in the face. My heart began pounding as I realized that I could not outrun the storm. Daydreams had led me wandering farther than I should have on such a threatening day. Now, with my crippled leg, I was trapped.

The goat bleated anxiously.

I heard my mother's voice again: "O-yu-na!"

But I had made my decision. With just one glance over my shoulder, I dropped the basket and slid upon sharp, skittering pebbles down the embankment.

"That was the last time I heard my mother's voice."

Even across the years the memory carried a fresh sadness and the old woman's words caught in her throat. She began to cough. The explosive, rattling noise made the round-sided mare snort in alarm, and for several minutes the dark stable echoed with an exchanging of gusts between human and horse. When at last her throat was clear, the old woman shook her head and, like the mare, snorted.

"Life is a funny thing, granddaughter," she said in a far-off voice. "You never know when you're doing something for the last time. One day—drinking tea with a good friend, chatting about this and that, and then—many years later—you look back and realize that that was the last time." She paused and lowered her gaze. Her voice quavered when she spoke again. "There was so much I wanted to say." Her trembling fingers pulled a jade pendant from the folds of her robe. The misty green stone was carved into the likeness of a galloping horse, its long mane and tail streaming in the wind. "I never got to thank my mother for this," she whispered.

The woman fell silent, her watery gray eyes staring vacantly into the night. The girl, still nestled beneath her grandmother's arm, waited respectfully, then prompted her to continue.

"What happened?" she whispered. There was no answer. "What happened?" she whispered again, her tone so urgent this time that even the white mare turned her black eyes upon the two and waited.

A change surged through the old woman. She stretched her hands before her, and the moonlight shone upon mottled flesh sagging from swollen joints. "These hands have done more good than my foot has bad, I tell you!" Anger rumbled in her words. Alarmed, the girl lifted her head from her grandmother's lap. "What was I to do?" the old woman asked into the darkness.

Wide-eyed now, the young girl could only swallow and timidly repeat, "What happened?"

The old hands dropped, disappearing into the robe's thick folds. "The goat and the kid lived. My mother died: lightning. Bad luck. Of course, my father and I were punished."

4. Lightning!

*M*y people fear lightning more than any of nature's powers. In spring and summer, without warning, bolts leap from the sky. They sting the earth's hide and capture for their own the spirits of our herdsmen and our animals. The rains they bring are welcome, of course, but such cruelty accompanying the gift! Who can count how many lives taken from the steppes? Hundreds to be sure, maybe even a thousand lives snatched from their families each season by lightning.

Once, when I was still very small, a summer storm arose midday, surprising the herdsmen of my *ail*. I was peeking out the door flap of our *ger* and still I can see the thorny bolt that scratched its way through the purple-black sky. Straight to earth it shot, crackling and snapping so loudly I jumped away from the door and pushed my fingers into my ears. Then a thunderous *bang!* that shook the ground beneath my feet. At once my mother grabbed my hand and out we rushed, she dragging me toward where the horses huddled. Others ran beside us, not caring about the wind throwing dirt and bits of leaves into our faces.

A strange burnt smell reached my nose even before we reached the horses. I remember my mother sweeping me up, trying to press my face to her chest. But I had already seen them: the lifeless bodies of three horses and two cousins sprawled grotesquely on the hillside. And I couldn't help it. Between my mother's splayed fingers I stared and stared at the blackened clothing, the singed manes and split hooves. And I couldn't stop shaking.

The night I helped the goat deliver her kid at the bottom of that creek bed, lightning crackled all around us. Each hissing bolt lit in my mind the stark picture of those hollow bodies—their spirits stolen by lightning. I was so scared! Then the heavens split open, pelting us with hail. With little Bator huddling in my lap and balls of ice piling at my feet, I hunched my shoulders against the pounding and fought to pull the slippery kid into this world. When the hail melted into a driving rain, still I was pushing and pulling, my hands bloody, my breath hot. At last my fingernails tore away the birth sac from the tiny black nose. The kid took his first panting breath. And I couldn't stop shaking.

Only then did I notice the brown water rising over my felt boots. We had to climb to higher ground—now! Lunging forward, I gathered the curly-coated kid into my arms, the sudden movement spilling Bator off my lap into the muddy water. Complaining in yowls, the kitten scampered up the embankment and huddled in the dark, watching. With the frightened kid bleating pitifully, and kicking so hard he almost unbalanced me, I managed to worm atop a large boulder. Swaying dangerously, I lifted the struggling animal above my head and shoved it over the bank's slippery edge. The mother goat, already on her feet, rushed after her newborn, using my lap as a stepping-stone to gain the brim in two leaps.

By the time I pulled myself, tumbling, up and over the embankment, my hands were bloodied, the fingernails torn and blackened. But we had made it. And just in time, too, for in the next instant I heard the water coming. Peering cautiously over the edge, I saw the foaming floodwaters pour over the boulder upon which I had just stood.

Later that night, when the storm had weakened to a steady rain and the goat and her kid had trotted off, bleating, into the darkness in search of the herd, I was still shaking. I had tucked Bator inside my *del* and the small heat from his little body against my chest became my focus as I stumbled in search of my own kin. Though my teeth chattered with cold and with fear, I was yet happy— happy that I had welcomed a new life into this world, happy that I had braved the lightning.

You should know, since some Mongol blood flows in your own veins, that *mong* means brave. That night I was proud to be Mongol.

"Oyuna!" I heard my father calling from the blackness ahead of me. "Oyuna! Where are you?"

"I'm coming," I called back. The frantic tone in his voice told my father's worry; that was my fault for staying out in the storm. But how happy he would be when I told him—

"Oyuna! You're all right!" My father's strong arms engulfed me, lifting me, feet dangling, right off the ground. He hugged my body so tightly that Bator wriggled out of my collar and leaped into the darkness to find his own way home. "Oh, Oyuna, Oyuna," my father cried. His shoulders heaved with great sobs. His embrace tightened still more. "I thought I had lost you, too."

Never before had I seen my father cry. It seemed a weakness then and I wanted him to stop. I wanted him to be brave, too. Struggling to free my head from his arms, I said, "Father, I'm all right. I was too far from our *ger* when the storm came upon us—upon Bator and me—and I knew with"—making a face, I jerked my head toward my crippled foot—"that I would be too slow back to camp. But Father, I have a surprise. I helped a goat to—"

"Oh, Oyuna, Oyuna," my father moaned, crushing my face into his arms again. Slowly he sank to the ground until I was standing, he kneeling. With his head now buried in my shoulders, my nose was pressed directly behind his ear and I remember thinking that that small crevice smelled exactly like the stiff, musty hairs between a dog's toes. To this day, whenever a dog places a paw in my lap . . . well, I remember that night and a great sadness sits upon my heart.

"Your mother is dead."

"No," I said, "she can't be. She isn't."

Looking blearily into my eyes, my father nodded. "The storm . . . the lightning." He spoke between gasping sobs. "Your mother went . . ."

". . . looking for me," I finished, the awful realization squeezing the life from my heart. It was my fault, then. She knew my twisted foot could not carry me swiftly to safety. And rather than try to limp back through the storm I had stayed with the goat. Now my mother was dead. My foot *was* bad luck.

By morning the blame for bringing lightning into our *ail* had been placed on both me and my father. And our animals. And all our possessions. We must have done something very bad, the clan's elders said, to so anger the gods that they would punish us with lightning. Now we were unclean.

While an uncle galloped off in search of a shaman to perform the cleansing ceremony, the women of my *ail* prepared to bury my mother.

Squatting, mute, on the cold, muddy ground, I watched them fasten a *del* of buttery yellow silk around my mother's stiff limbs. Over her arms they slid a long matching vest decorated with fancy stitching. Across her scarf was fitted a heavy silver cap from which dangled shining braids of black hair along with gleaming silver pendants studded with yellow amber and blue sapphires. I had never seen her dressed so elegantly. This was how she looked the day she married my father, I was told.

Then the women dug a hole in the ground and laid my mother in it. Beside her were laid her saddle, her food bowl, a cooking pot filled with water and mutton, and a block of tea leaves. I was glad at least that she would have food in the next world. Then a dun-colored mare and her nursing foal were led to the hole. With a strong blow to the forehead, each fell to its knees, dead. Both bodies were pulled into the hole and laid beside the body of my mother. Now she would always have milk to drink. After the dirt was piled on top of the bodies and the sod patted into place, my mother's favorite horse, a gray mare, was killed. The meat was set aside for the evening dinner, while the hide was stuffed with dried grasses. The huge, wobbling apparition was then impaled upon a long pole angling toward the sky. My mother would not be left to walk in the next world.

Half a day later, still mute, I found myself seated beside my father in our oxcart. Our *ail* was moving a short distance away from the freshly mounded earth—to a safer place. I kept looking over my shoulder, watching my mother's grave grow smaller. The afternoon's brisk wind sifted through the dead horse's mane. And the hide, still soft, rippled, almost as if muscles bunched and released beneath it. I wondered if my mother's spirit was already galloping toward the next world.

The shaman, robed in white and carrying a drum and a staff that sprouted a hairy oxtail, met us in the next valley. Under his thunderous directions, two huge fires were lit. To the pounding of his drum, a lance was thrust into the ground beside each fire and a long rope tied between them. On this rope dangled stuffed felt dolls, one for each of the gods whose blessing we needed. Already my relatives had picked up the chant.

My father and I waited on our oxcart, packed with the few possessions belonging to us. We had left our *ger* behind, sitting alone on the steppe, holding only my mother's bed and a few of her old clothes. No one would dare to touch these unclean objects. They were left for the winds to wash through them and, over time, to carry them away. My father had even taken the jade pendant from my neck and thrown it into the mud before hurrying me onto the oxcart.

The women of our clan stood in a double line between us and the fires. They also waited, chanting, heads turned in the direction of the shaman. I was cradling a shivering Bator in my arms, covering his eyes to keep him from bolting. The old white-robed man signaled for silence and, when only the crackling of the fires could be heard, shook his tasseled staff high in the air.

My father spoke to our ox once, then again, sharply, for the animal was swinging its head nervously from side to side and bellowing loudly. Each time it tipped its long horns I could see the rolling white of its eye. Finally, with another of my father's shouts, the animal pushed into its harness, still swinging its horns, and the women began chanting again and flinging water at us. Under the rope we passed. One of the felt dolls just brushed my head, raising prickles of fear on my arms. From the corner of my eye, I saw the god of long journeys, an eagle feather lashed to its black felt body, bobbing crazily above my head. Queasiness flooded my stomach. What did this mean?

But there was no time for another worry, for now we were passing between the two fires. Our ox bellowed in fear. The heat sucked at my skin. The moment we cleared the orange flames Bator squeezed out from my arms and fled into the grasses. I climbed off the cart and, through several more trips, helped my father drive our horses, sheep, and goats under the rope and between the two fires. It is no easy task coaxing animals toward fire, let me assure you, and by the time the shaman pronounced us cleansed the sun was already setting and I was covered with sweat.

That night our clan feasted with the shaman and laughed and sang as if all were right with the world.

But my father and I were left to lie upon our backs under the stars. An arm's length from him, I saw that the fleece covers pulled high across his face shook erratically. And muffled moans, like those from a wounded animal, crept from the pile to die in the dark.

Where were my tears? Sleepless, I threw aside my covers and stumbled away. My feet found the crushed grass paths left by the wheels of the oxcarts. Numbly, while the moon arced overhead, I followed the wet tracks back to the lonely *ger* upon the steppe. As I neared it I began to tremble. But a need pushed me closer. Finally, keeping one wary eye on the gray horse apparition that leaped motionlessly toward the sky, I fell to my knees and searched through the grasses surrounding my mother's grave. When my fingers closed on the small jade pendant, tears burst from my eyes. All the way back to camp I sobbed, clutching the little horse given to me by my mother. By the time I slipped back under my covers, the pendant again tied around my neck, though hidden within my *del*, the sky was growing pale. Exhausted but still sleepless, I could only stare, swollen-eyed, at the few floating stars and blame myself.

The next day, when our *ail* moved on, our oxcart and all of our animals were forced to the back of the line. That day and those that followed, our horses and sheep and goats ate the grass trampled by others.

And so it went for the next three moons. Always my father and I were the last to choose a site for the small *ger* we had pieced together from discards, the last to dip water from the stream. My relatives were friendly, even consoling me over my mother's death, though no one dared touch me, or hug me.

How I missed my mother then! My heart hung like a stone weight banging in my chest.

I worked hard just to walk in her shadow. Rising before dawn, I gathered dung, started the cooking fire, boiled tea, and milked our mares. After my father left the *ger,* I combed the goats, stirred the *ayrag,* churned the butter, and milked the mares again. But as hard as I tried, the *tarag* burned, the *aaruul* turned moldy, and the mutton was stringy and tasteless. Day after day I met with failure and I heaped blame on the bad luck of my foot. I began to feel the bad luck hovering over me like a cat over a mousehole, waiting to pounce.

And always at dusk my father sat silent, his eyes cast down.

5. Flight

*T*he horses saved me then.

No longer at dusk, but well after dark I waited. Until dinner was eaten and the bowls wiped clean. Until my father had smoked his pipe and fallen asleep. Until, holding my breath, I could slip into the night.

Searching, my hands found thick mane, and I lifted my weight from the ground. Kicked wildly to free myself. Knees found their familiar niche behind warm ropes of muscle. An urgent whisper into the hollow of an understanding ear, and striped hooves carried me away.

I don't know across how many hills, beneath how many stars we sped each night. Bent over the horse's powerful neck, my shoulders heaved with sadness, rose and fell with each thundering stride. I shed salty tears, lifting first one cheek and then the other that the wind might lick them dry.

Night after night across the darkened breast of Itugen, the earth goddess, we galloped. But I couldn't escape it.

My bad luck I carried with me, clamped to the horse's side. And, slowly, I let my heart unwind behind me, leaving it in thin strips to dry and twist in the next sun.

At last in the moonlight I sat, a shadow on the horizon, staring at the silent *gers*. And I vowed that if ever I had the chance, I would carry my bad luck far, far away.

6. The Night Brings Surprises

*A*fter three months walking at the tail of our caravan, my father found another wife.

All during that third moon I had known that some trouble was eating at him, although he still rarely spoke to me, only asking me twice during that time to cook for him the intestines of wolves he had hunted. My mother had taught me long ago that eating the insides of a wolf heals a painful stomach. After all, the wolf can devour anything—from blades of grass to a many-days-dead sheep—and never suffer. Therefore I willingly cut into pieces and cooked in boiling water the slippery intestines my father handed me so that his aching stomach would gain the wolf's strength. And while I stirred the bubbling broth I wondered what my father was keeping from me. At summer's end, with the sheep shorn and goats combed, the woolly bundles piled high inside our *ger* awaiting trade, my father broke his silence.

"The mutton tastes especially good tonight, Oyuna,"

he said. That was when I braced my shoulders for his news, for although I had dug up some wild onions that day to add to the stew, my tongue had already told me that the meat I had prepared was as flavorless as always. I watched my father swirl his hand in the cooking pot, pulling out a greasy chunk of meat and plopping it directly into his mouth. He chewed noisily and swallowed. Then, in the firelight, his lips spread in a toothy grin. A dog grins in the same manner, drawing back its lips and hanging its head—tail thumping hopefully—when it has run behind your back and nipped an unsuspecting lamb.

"I have a surprise for you," he said, beginning haltingly. "No, Oyuna, I count again. As surely as the camel carries twin humps upon his back, I have two surprises!" His voice was rising with excitement. "First, I am going to . . . No, that must follow. First, Oyuna, I tell you that next moon you travel with me to Karakorum for the festival."

My father sat back, tall and proud, watching the excitement bring light to my face as the morning sun bathes the land with its warm glow.

Karakorum! My mind galloped dizzily. Year after year I had listened to the stories brought back by those who had visited the great walled city—the only place of its kind on the steppes. A palace once used by the Khan himself stood there, in the purple shadows of the Hangay Mountains and guarded by a giant stone tortoise the size of a horse. Tents of all colors spread in every direction, some big enough to cover a thousand heads! And in the center, a tree crafted of silver with four golden snakes wrapping its trunk. All you had to do, I had been told, was speak to this tree, telling it which drink would quench your thirst, and from the mouth of a serpent would pour *ayrag* or wine or the honeyed *boal,* directly into a silver cup. And now I, Oyuna of the Kerait tribe, would travel to see those wonders with my own eyes!

"And next, daughter . . ." My father began speaking again, then closed his mouth, tapping his wooden bowl sharply on the rim of the cooking pot to gain my attention. I struggled to shake my head clear.

"Yes! I am listening," I said.

"And next, daughter," he continued, "I tell you my other surprise: not many more days will you cook alone." He sat back once more, grinning, waiting for the understanding to show itself upon my face. But impatience saddled him that night and when my face remained blank my father leaned forward to add words. "I have found a new wife," he said, "a new mother for you." Quickly he began to scoop dripping chunks of meat into his mouth, one after the other, his brown eyes glancing both nervously and hopefully across the fire into my face.

I felt its excited smile grow cold. Spirits that had been soaring toward Karakorum dropped to the hard earth. "A new mother," he had said. I didn't want a new mother. My mother was dead.

I wanted, then, to race out of the *ger.* Instead, nodding stiffly at my father's words, I calmly rose.

As if from a distance I watched my hand wipe the meat from my bowl back into the cooking pot. Without licking it clean, I set the bowl aside. Turning, I fastened my gaze hard onto the smooth wooden handle of the ladle as it dipped water into another bronze pot. Feet moved beneath me as the pot was carried to the fire and set in the coals to boil. With my back toward my father once again, I spent many blurry-eyed minutes on my knees, searching for the bag of tea leaves. The silence within the *ger* was so complete I could hear the silk fabric across my chest rustling with my every rapid breath.

My father went on eating, finishing his meal without speaking again. Finally he licked his bowl clean and set it aside. Then he lit his pipe. The *ger* thickened with smoke and unspoken thoughts.

I sat across the fire, staring vacantly past my father at the blue and white pattern in a saddle rug. I longed to escape, to rinse myself in the cold night air upon the back of a horse, to think about this news. Looking up, I saw the moon traveling across the round scrap of sky framed by the *ger*'s smoke hole. Would my father never go to sleep?

Puff after puff he sat beside the fire: face solemn, thinking, relighting his pipe, and thinking some more. Desperate for a task to harness my restless thoughts, I pulled a torn *del* onto my lap and began to sew.

"There follows yet another surprise, Oyuna." The words made me jump. My father's voice was quiet now. His happiness seemed to have fled.

When I looked across the fire at him, the hard planes of his face had softened. He appeared almost shy. This time he spoke with his chin lowered, which muffled his words, and I had to tip my ear toward him.

"At the festival—" My father coughed, then spent several long seconds clearing his throat. My heart was pounding. "At the festival," he continued at last, "I will speak with the Ongirrat tribe about a mate for you, too, Oyuna." If it seemed that my spirits had plummeted to the cold earth before, they now shattered in icy splinters. "You are twelve, I think. It is past time. And there are no better people with horses than the Ongirrat. Why else would they carry the name of the swift, chestnut-colored horses they breed? You, too, daughter, have a way with the horses. You will add to their wealth."

My father was fumbling inside his *del* while he spoke. Short grunts punctuated his search. Then he motioned with his pipe hand for me to come closer. Hesitantly I rose and limped a path around the fire. I squatted, lopsided, next to him, my own chin now buried in my chest. I saw my father's fist open. In his palm, shimmering in the firelight, lay my dowry: long silver earrings ablaze with coral and mother-of-pearl.

"I will do my best for you, Oyuna," my father said. "I will do my best to make you a good match. But you understand . . ." He searched for words, trying to keep his passive gaze fixed upon the stricken face of his only daughter—trying not to let his gaze fall past my waist. His voice trailed off as his eyes could not. Clumsily, his large hands pushed the clinking earrings into my small palms. One by one he closed my fingers around them. Then we sat, father and daughter, his hand upon mine, in the silence of our *ger*. Tears welled in my eyes as well as his, but no one blinked. We each understood. With my crippled leg, any match would be a difficult one.

No! No! No! the words screamed in my head. I tried to bolt, but my legs wouldn't move.

For endless snaking moments my father and I sat beside the fire. He finally released my hand just long enough to wrap his arm around my shoulders, to pull me closer. The motion was stiff, unused as my father was to giving the hugs and kisses of a mother. That night I tried to accept his offering, but I was numb. And at last, after huddling beneath his shoulder for many long breaths, counting the hurried puffs from the pipe that measured the uneasiness of us both, I gently lifted my father's arm from my shoul-

ders and returned to the other side of the fire. Dropping
the earrings into my lap, I picked up my sewing and began
pushing the needle through the padded silk. Instantly I
stabbed my finger. The sharpness let spill down my cheeks
the tears that had been pushing into my eyes. My shoulders sank, trembling, as I sucked the salty wound.

"I will give you a horse as well, Oyuna. One of your
own choosing." I could not at first comprehend the words
that drifted through the haze. But as their meaning became
clear to me, I felt my sadness begin to rise out of the *ger*
with the fire's smoke. "You may choose a horse at the
festival," my father was saying, "from the ones brought
to be sold or traded. I am planning on buying some new
mares anyway. So you may choose a horse, too. Any horse
you want, Oyuna. It is my gift."

Through streaming tears I gaped at my father's face.
Beneath its leathery mask I now saw an awkward tenderness and knew in my heart that for all his seeming clumsi-
ness, my father was doing his best to care for me. Just as
awkwardly I lurched around the fire, surprising him by
throwing my arms around his neck and almost choking
him with my happiness. Hands waving in mock agony,
my father groaned and yelped and bellowed. But when
he was free to duck his head and relight his pipe, the fire's
glow upon his face showed that he knew, at last, he had
done well.

Finding no words, I could only squeal and hug my
father again. Then I whirled and plunged through the
door flap, pushing my way into the clear cold night and
drinking in the fresh, raw air. Already I was picturing the
horse I would choose—the swiftest horse on the steppes.
My mind was racing. What was my horse doing now? I
wondered. What was he thinking about? From somewhere

out in the darkness a horse whinnied. My heart rose in answer, its joy spilling forth in an exuberant shout that rushed across the land into the night.

A soft whinny came from the round-bellied mare. Stepping close to the two humans murmuring in her stall, she lowered her neck to breathe in their smell. Then she pulled back, swung her head up and down vigorously, and resumed her restless circling, small hooves sifting through the dried grasses in measured rustling.

"She likes your story, I think," the girl said, eyes resting proudly upon the beautiful horse. She laid her head in her grandmother's lap. "How long was it until you chose your horse?"

The old woman closed her eyes. A happy smile stretched the thin lips. "To tell you the truth, granddaughter, I cannot even remember the days between my father's news and our arrival at Karakorum. I can't even tell you how many of my relatives traveled with us, although I'm sure some must have remained behind to tend to the herds." She cupped her hands before her in the darkness. "My mother used to say, 'When happiness settles upon you like a butterfly, sit very quiet and remember the colors.' " She opened her eyes.

"And that is what I remember about my journey to the festival: the many colors shimmering around me. The glint of ice slipping from a brilliant purple aster, the brown matting of withered feather grasses crackling beneath the cart wheels, one emerald green

valley that sheltered a stream. Every afternoon, a pink
sky dotted with bronze clouds. Always ahead,
puffing larger each day yet still cheating us at dusk,
squatted hazy blue mountains.

"And it seemed that good luck rode beside us. As
we passed a reedy lake one day, my fingers counted
seven sawbills and I at first caught my breath, but then
two more of the black-backed birds broke the water,
making a lucky nine. Another time, I spied a silvery
wolf far ahead of us in the dusk. He was laying good
fortune across our path with each silent footfall. And
every night, sitting beneath the stars, I watched the
golden moon swell fuller with its bounty.

"At last, beneath a lavender twilight sky, we paused
upon a rise overlooking the festival. From all
directions lumbered glowing white, *ger*-laden oxcarts,
pinning themselves in great hems around the city
that was Karakorum."

7. Noises

Sounds of laughing and fighting and singing filtered through the thick felt walls of our *ger* the whole night. On my bed I flipped and flopped like a fish on a cold riverbank. So excited!—for somewhere on the dark steppe grazed the horse I would choose as my own. And so scared!—for somewhere in the surrounding *gers* slept the boy who might agree to choose me. By early morning, with small strummings of music still reaching my ears, I gave up trying to sleep.

My father still slept in his bed, so, as quietly as I could, I set about preparing the morning meal. The door flap brushed my back as I reached outside to loosen the felt collar protecting the *ger*'s smoke hole. Then I slipped back inside and poked at the fire's embers, adding a few small pieces of dung from the basket. I poured out the last of the water we had carried with us, then set it to boil in a bronze pot and, when it bubbled furiously, threw in a handful of tea leaves. Right away I pulled the pot from the flames to let the tea rest while I stepped outside again, dragging a big leather bag.

The few horses we had brought with us were hobbled a short way from our *ger*. The bag thudded softly on my hip as I picked my way through the dark, stepping lightly on the wet grasses already flattened by hundreds of feet. As I neared the area set aside for grazing, a thick fog rose waist-high and I had to search through many horses until I recognized ours. I was surprised to find that three of our horses were missing and that two new mares were hobbled beside our small herd, a puffy triangle—the brand of my clan—already burned into each mare's right shoulder. My father must have made a late-night trade, I thought. And I would soon be adding another new horse to our herd, a swift one of my very own! An excited shiver tickled my back.

Pushing my way through the furry bodies, I found our brown mare with the white foot and gently shouldered aside her large colt long enough to squeeze a good serving of milk into the leather bag. Then, patting him on the rump as he shoved past to suckle again noisily, I retraced my wet path through the darkness back to our *ger*.

My father was still asleep when I returned, so I poured myself a small bowl of tea, added some of the warm mare's milk and a chunk of butter to it, and sat by the fire thinking about the beautiful horse I would choose today. Would it be silver gray or shining black?

Would he be fat or thin? my mind interrupted, reminding me of the day's other choosing. My stomach went cold. Pushing that unpleasant thought from my mind, I concentrated on the goodness the day held. Would I choose a mare or a gelding?

Would he be young or old? my mind interrupted again.

My stomach twisted. To be married to an old, smelly man would be horrible. But, as if with a heat of its own, I felt the misshapen foot curled beneath me and knew that no young, good-looking boy would choose me.

By the time my father opened his eyes, rolling over and groaning loudly, I was all churned up inside with both excitement and fear.

"Father," I said, my heart pounding, "can I go choose a horse now? One of my very own?" I handed him his bowl of tea with mare's milk, no butter. And do you know what he did? As slowly as if this were any ordinary day, he just yawned and stretched and grinned.

"What do you think about our new mares?" he said. "I would guess you have found them by now." His brown eyes were twinkling at me across the bowl he lifted to his mouth.

Truthfully, I could not even remember the colors of the new mares, but I said to my father, "They're beautiful. Both of them. Now can I go choose a horse? Please?" A worry inside me nagged that, even though the day was just turning light, my champion horse, the one meant just for me, was already being led away by someone else.

My father smiled. Then he dressed. And then he went out. "An important messenger from the Naiman tribe may be visiting," he told me, grinning sheepishly. "You must wait here until I return."

And so, penned apart from where my heart already lay, I felt as if that morning trickled by like the last drops from a dried-up goat. I left the *ger* only long enough to refill our water bags in the nearby Orhon River, lugging them back through the crowds of happy people buying and trading for all that would give them pleasure. Angry, I put extra force into beating the leather bag of *ayrag*.

With reckless energy I sewed haphazard stitches into a stirrup leather that had torn during our journey to Karakorum. Not even looking to see who passed, I tossed yesterday's stew out the door, filled the cauldron with water, and set it to boiling a large sheep's leg. And then I paced, one lurching circle after another, around the fire. Now, I didn't tell you that I had brought my cat, Bator, with me to the festival, but let me say that he just crouched nervously on my bed the whole morning, round eyes staring yellow-green at my unbridled fretting.

Midday came and went and I finally poured a bowl of broth with little bits of mutton in it, downing just a few sips before giving up and letting Bator lick the bowl clean. The heat of the day was growing inside the *ger*. By the time my father stumbled in, his grin even wider, it was midafternoon. Quickly I poured him a bowl of the mutton stew, handed him a piece of *khuruud,* and begged again to leave. So lost was he in his own happiness that he waved me away without speaking.

The blue roan that my father had been riding stood tethered outside, so I pulled myself into the saddle. The fat horse grunted as I kicked him into a jarring trot toward Karakorum's north gate, where the festival horses were grouped for sale or trade.

As I circled Karakorum's mud walls, bouncing closer to the north gate, my mouth opened in amazement. There were so many horses! I counted five tethered rows of twenty horses each in front of me, which would be a hundred horses, and I could see at least two more sets of a hundred beyond them. Their sleek rumps, tails swishing lazily in the sunshine, stretched in brown and black and gray waves endlessly before me. Heart thumping wildly, I started down the first row.

Almost instantly my heart sank. For riding between

the rows, I counted many empty spaces on the ropes: the best horses had already been led away. After all, the festival had been going on for three days now, and for my people, few activities held more pleasure than horse trading. I sighed. So these were the leftovers, the ones nobody wanted.

But a small determination started within me. My father was a noted horse breeder. The foals of our old spotted stallion were valued all across the steppes. And my mother had been an excellent rider, with an eye for a good horse as well. Surely their daughter could find one horse in these hundreds that had been overlooked, one horse that I could train to be a racing champion. You see, I was remembering the boy and his brown horse I had seen as a child—the champions with the sky blue scarf of good luck. And I was remembering how my mother had watched that boy's mother. And I was deciding right then and there that this was how I would capture some good luck: I would carefully choose just the right horse, train it day upon day until it could gallop the morning without so much as a deep breath, and then, next fall, return to the festival to win the long race.

So, shading my eyes from the bright August sun, I held the roan to a bit-champing, short-stepping walk, frowning at first one and then another potential winner. Occasionally I fingered my mother's jade horse pendant, trying to remember everything I had learned about choosing a good horse: the slope of the shoulder, the length of the back, the angle of the hip. And gradually my excitement returned. How surprised everyone would be, how proud my father would be, I thought, when I won next year's long race with a "leftover."

Ahead of me a reddish brown back rose past its neighbors and I reined in to examine an extraordinarily tall animal. Four black stockings wrapped beautifully straight legs, but the bony hips jutting against a dull coat mimicked the distant Hangay Mountains. Needs a little fattening, I thought, but he's a possibility. Loosening the reins and clucking, I moved on.

My gaze passed over sorrels and duns and pintos. The sunny blond mane of a high-spirited chestnut filly made me stop again. She was young, probably not having seen two whole years, and the strange odors and noises were making her prance and snort. Already a cloud of dust blurred the brilliant white splashing her face and forefeet. How easily I pictured myself astride her in my red silk *del,* matching strides with the antelope darting across the steppes. What a racing team we would make! Surely she could be a champion.

But I just had to see all the horses, so, squeezing my legs, I pushed the roan on. Past grays and goldens. Past blacks and bays. I disregarded the ones with sagging backs or swollen legs. I shook my head at the mare with the hazy eye and the gelding who yawned, revealing crooked teeth.

Rounding the last row of horses, I had almost decided on the young chestnut filly when shrill squeals burst from a knot of horses tethered ahead. Already a cloud of yellow dust swirled around the kicking and biting animals. The roan came instantly to life, snorting anxiously.

Now, I remember this next part as clearly as the blue morning sky. From out of that cloud of dust came these words: "Help me away from here!"

Well, at the terrified sound of those words I urged my roan into a bounding gallop. Even before reining him to a stop I slid off, plunging into the dust storm stirred up by angry hooves. I knew the only smart thing to do was to approach this squabble from the front, so I ducked under the tether and then, rather bravely, I might add, shoved my way between the sweating bodies. Scolding and slapping at what turned out to be three horses, I finally stopped the kicking, though ears remained pinned, teeth bared.

Coughing, I searched under the bellies for the person that had called for help. But there was no one. Forward and back I walked, peering through the dust for what must be a trampled body. But I couldn't find anything. The horses stood more calmly now and I patted one of them on the rump, thinking. The frightened person must have already escaped, I decided, and run back toward the festival. It was probably one of the younger boys who took pride in testing his skill against unbroken horses. I shook my head in disgust and, as long as I was there, stepped back to examine the three.

All were mares. The one on the left was a plump sorrel with a star almost hidden beneath her shaggy forelock. In the center was a ragged old white mare who had taken the brunt of the beating. Her far hind leg was hitched up painfully, blood trailing a red streak through her dirty yellow coat. The mare on the right was a dappled gray, middle-aged, with a shiny black mane and tail. She was trim and well muscled and I mentally added her to the list of possibilities.

Pitying the beaten-up old white mare, I worked my way down her side to examine the injured leg. She was hopping around painfully, still fearful of the horses on either side of her. The leg wasn't broken, so I moved back to her head. Grasping her halter, I spoke to her for a few minutes, trying to calm her. She responded immediately, lowering her muzzle and blowing softly into my arms. Her black eyes looked directly into mine.

Help me away from here. Those same words formed in

my head as clearly as if I had heard them spoken. But I *had* to have heard them spoken, I thought. Still grasping the halter, I looked carefully over my left shoulder, then over my right. I saw no one nearby.

The sun was warm for late August and sweat ran down my back. Yet a cold chill prickled the skin on my arms. I stared into the mare's eyes, doubting. Her eyes looked back at mine, into mine. And I heard the words again. *Help me away from here.*

I stumbled backward. My level head told me it had to be a trick. And then I knew. Kokochu! That was it! The great shaman Kokochu lived within the walls of Karakorum. He could make spirits talk, make people see things that weren't real. It was a joke. He was having fun with me.

Trying to hide my embarrassment, I walked as straight as I could on my crippled leg toward the fat blue roan, again dozing in the sun. My hands were still shaking as I gathered the reins and a hank of mane and pulled myself into the saddle. As we moved off, something made me turn.

And there was the white mare, her head straining against the tether to look at me. Eyes eager, ears pricked forward, she whinnied frantically.

Suddenly the horses around me swayed back and forth, duns blending into browns blending into bays blending into blackness. The heat, I thought, clutching for the arching front of my father's saddle. Get out of the heat. Blindly, I pushed the roan into his jarring trot and headed, I hoped, toward our *ger*. But as clearly as the sun cuts through the clouds, the words formed in my head even as I retreated: *Help me.*

8. The White Mare

*F*rom the tailboard of our oxcart, with Bator snuggled beside me, I watched Karakorum grow smaller. Winter was whispering its coming on the back of a raw wind that bit at my cheeks and nose. Below my dangling feet, the dried grasses shivered in the pale half-light of a hazy sun. The festival was over. All across the steppes, *ger*-laden oxcarts were drifting, like giant white butterflies, away from the walled city. Each carried with it a sampling of the great city's nectar. Champion archers clutched new bows. A wrestler beamed beneath the hard-won title of Arslan, "Lion." I had watched with envy as a young girl upon her prancing bay horse was showered with silk scarves, surrounded by an approving crowd. She had won this year's long race, even beating the older boys. I had had to swallow hard and force my heart to wish her well. But how I longed to place my feet in those stirrups.

Dwarfed by the cart's towering load, I sat with my back pressing into it, just listening to the farewell shouts, the oiled wheels creaking, the ox grunting. And thinking about prizes.

My father was carrying home his prize. Hands upon the reins, he talked and laughed with his new wife, while her two sons sat wordless behind them. My father had been unable to award me. While a brief sadness darkened his face in the telling, I had quietly sighed with relief. And for my own prize? I stared at the braided brown rope clutched in my fist. My eyes followed its looping arc, swaying with the rhythm of the wagon, down, then back up and around the bobbing head of the white mare. Yes, limping behind us was my choice, my champion. The white mare.

But I had had to choose her, hadn't I? She had spoken to me. Although I could hardly explain this to my father.

"Oyuna," he had said sadly, shaking his head as we stood beside the white mare and her owner. "Are you sure this is the horse you want?"

I had nodded, though hesitantly enough to show my own uncertainty. My father was looking into the mare's mouth. "How many winters?" he asked her owner.

"Only seven," the man answered.

"Hmph!" my father grunted. "Closer to twelve if she's seen one." He was walking around her then, running his hands along the white legs already fuzzy with a winter coat. When he saw the bloodstained hind leg he bent for a closer look. "Trot her out!" he ordered abruptly.

The owner tugged on the halter until the mare reluctantly stumbled into a painfully unbalanced trot. I cringed as my father's scowl fell upon me. "Why do you choose a crippled animal, Oyuna? You know better! Who would pay silver for such?"

But the white mare was being led back to me, her dark

eyes looking into mine. My father was right. Who would pay dear silver for a cripple?

"No one," I answered quietly. "Because no one would pay silver for me." Looking into my father's face, I saw that he flushed. "But this is the horse that I choose."

Grumbling, and still shaking his head, my father quickly counted out silver coins and the man handed me the mare's lead rope. We walked back to our *ger* in silence.

Every day since then I had searched the black eyes of the mare and waited for her to speak again. But there was only silence. And it had been five days now.

At that moment the mare stumbled, nearly jerking the rope from my hands before she regained her balance. Tears blurred my eyes as I thought how I had wasted my chance for a champion on an old, crippled horse that could barely plod to the pace of an ox. She wasn't even suited for breeding, I now knew, for after the silver had changed hands her seller admitted he had had no foals from her.

The pale sun crept across the arching sky, then slowly began sinking toward earth. Still I stared into the black eyes of the white mare. She was staring back at me now, steadily, but no words filled my head. All I heard was a small explosion of laughter from the front of the cart, then the same rhythmic creaking of heavy wheels and straining harness. The hard beating of grouses' wings reached my ears as a pair was flushed from beneath the cart's path. Then I heard the soft cry of cranes somewhere in the distance. Between my own heartbeats, which suddenly pounded in my ears, I thought I even heard the water rippling away from one crane's plunge after a fish. And then, as I held my breath near to bursting in amazement, the even softer scurry of tiny mouse feet through the grasses tickled my ears. The animals of the steppes, even though hidden from my eyes, were suddenly made known to me by their loud bustling. The grasslands were practically roaring with hooves tromping, wings flapping, claws digging, bills snapping.

At last, blue-faced, I'm sure, I let my breath out in a rush and sucked in lungfuls of fresh air. Blood raced through my veins. My shoulders shook. Already panicky, I startled when the corner of my eye caught the flashing white tail of a bounding rabbit. Glancing to the right, I instantly picked out the stone-still squat of a well-camouflaged *suslik* and, to my surprise and fear, I saw crouching directly behind the little squirrel, not more than a good leap from our oxcart, a yellow-eyed, grinning fox. My eyes darted to the left. Deep within the grasses, clinging to a swaying stem, perched a leathery grasshopper. A fat beetle beneath it crawled through the shadows striping the hard dirt. Had these creatures always been so close? Why had I never spotted them before?

I flinched even before I saw them: a dozen *saiga* antelope spilling down a far hill. The white mare snorted, dancing sideways to watch with me. My heart doubled its beat. I tensed; fingernails cut into my palms. Somehow I wanted to leap from the cart and race with them.

What was happening to me? Why did the world suddenly seem so loud, so wild? I squeezed my eyes shut and focused on calming my breathing. Slowly I sucked in the cool air, pushed it evenly out over my pursed lips. Again, I breathed in, rhythmically, slowly. In and out. Steady. Easy.

The faint moldy odor of cheese reached my nostrils. It must have been coming from the felt-wrapped package I had placed in the cart's front seat. I thought I could even make out the sweet smell of the millet flour in a bag slumped beside it. But how could that be? Curious, I sucked in the deepest breath I could hold. This time countless smells swept through me, even, I was certain, the salty sweat beading on the wide pink nostrils of our ox. Somewhere below us I could sniff the days-old droppings of an animal I couldn't name. Eyes still closed, I inhaled the peppery fragrance of wildflowers mixed with the light scent of moisture-filled grasses. That made my tongue grow wet. I inhaled a coolness. Frowning, I breathed in again. Yes, I could taste it. Turning my head west, toward a fading sun shedding its warm glow upon my eyelids, I opened my eyes. The white mare was already looking at the same dusty shallow my gaze had fixed upon. Water! Somehow I just knew it was there. I had already smelled it and tasted it. At least, I thought I had.

I called to my father, hollering the words over the swaying bulk of our cart. I heard him call to the others. The oxen slowed, then swung toward the sinking sun.

How had I known?

The white mare was calmer now, bobbing her head with each step. And again she was looking at me. I studied the black eyes, encircled in white lashes, and it occurred to me that they were twinkling. The mare, it seemed, was enjoying a private joke. She was laughing at me! There were no words in my head. Just sounds. And sights I had never seen. And tastes. And smells.

9. In the GER of Echenkorlo

On a clear wintry morning, five months after the festival, the *ger* of Echenkorlo, my shamaness grandmother, appeared. I had spotted it at dawn, small and black, seated alone by the frozen stream, well apart from my *ail*'s clusters of white. But when I pushed my head back inside our *ger* to shout the news to my waking father, he hissed at me, forbidding me to approach the grandmother I had not seen since my mother was alive.

"Her mind is twisted," he said, spitting into the cooking fire. "Too many years traveling alone." He snorted— "Selfish fool!"— as he bundled into a heavy blue *del,* its hood trimmed in the stiff black and gray fur of the wolf. "Echenkorlo should journey with the tribe," he growled. Then, pointing a finger at me, "You don't see a bird flying apart from the flock, do you? Or a marmot tunneling in a direction of its own choosing?"

Shuraa, my father's new wife, worked around us silently, not taking sides.

Arguing with my father was always a mistake, yet once again that didn't stop me. And so my retort began, "But the eagle flies alone—"

"Echenkorlo is no eagle," my father shouted, stomping outside with his saddle in his arms. "She is but a silly old woman who has confused her dreams for her travels." Even in the morning's cold, his stubby fingers darted about the braided horsehair fittings, expertly fastening the saddle upon the back of a dozing horse. Hastily he mounted and kicked the horse into a grunting leap.

But I had already decided that I would see my grandmother. I had questions for her, questions that only she could answer. My stubborn anger rose to meet my father's and in its heat I shoved my chin forward and whispered at his back, "You can't keep me from seeing her." As if my words had flown to his ears, my father instantly spun his horse and trotted back to my side. Surprised, I stood speechless while my father sat in his saddle, thinking. White puffs of vapor rose silently from the horse's glistening nostrils. Then my father spoke, in a voice almost as quiet as my whisper, and just as firm.

"Echenkorlo is your mother's mother—your only grandmother still walking this earth. It is right you should see her, Oyuna, but not alone, for she is . . . different. You must wait until I walk with you. Do you hear me, Oyuna? You are not safe with her alone."

His dark eyes held mine, waiting. I nodded, slowly, for a sudden uneasiness at the pit of my stomach had chilled my desire to run toward the small *ger* by the stream, even in my father's company. And so, when my father galloped away, I took but one more quick glance at that silent *ger* before ducking inside our own.

All that day I worked at stirring and sewing in silence,

though my mind buzzed with questions. My mother had spoken of her own mother, Echenkorlo, on few occasions, and we had seen her even more rarely. But I did know she was a shamaness and I knew shamans possessed the answer to any question. So what I longed to ask her more than anything was this: Where would I find a swift horse?

Anxiously I waited for my father's return, thrusting my head through the door flap after the completion of each task to make sure my grandmother's *ger* was still there. But by late afternoon my father had still not left the herds. Shuraa was also away, milking the goats. Both the sun and the temperature were dropping rapidly, and though an icy shiver tickled up and down my back, I could rein in my curiosity no longer. I threw the leather water bag over my shoulder and meandered toward the stream.

A thin snow powdered the ground, so the hawks soaring above could see that my tracks snaked behind me in indecision. First toward the stream, then toward the *ger,* then— in a moment of chill fear—curving back toward my father's *ger,* yet again doubling back toward Echenkorlo's. At last I stood within its shadow, cautiously pressing my ear to the felt wall. In that hush that comes at the end of the day I could almost hear the earth spirits babbling beneath the frozen roof of their watery pathway. Their running chatter mingled with the moaning of the rising afternoon wind, and then other voices, human voices cackling and singing within the *ger,* reached my ear. And next, at once, as if all nature had caught me listening, everything was still. Heart trapped, thumping, in my throat, I silently turned to tiptoe away.

"Please don't keep us waiting, Oyuna." A singsong voice, ripe with power, spoke from within the felt walls. "Your tea grows cold." I jumped in my snow tracks, suddenly remembering that my mother had said that Echenkorlo could often "see" without seeing.

A different voice then, one high and brittle, like ice splintering across a creek, spoke through the walls. "Your tea grows cold . . . ," it echoed, then, cackling wildly, ". . . and your toe grows green!" The raucous laughter of ravens spilled from the *ger.*

Words inside my head screamed at me to run, run back to the safety of my own *ger,* but —how strange this was!— instead I calmly placed a hand upon the heavy door flap, alive with leaping animals in every color, and pushed it aside. How carefully I lifted my booted foot high over the raised doorsill, for to stumble upon it was to step on the neck of the *ger's* owner and an instinct deep within me warned not to offend the inhabitants of this *ger.*

As the door flap whooshed shut against my back, I fell to the woven wool *shirdiks,* my hands pressing my face, gagged and blinded by thick smoke. Scented with the perfume of some plant unknown to me, the smoke lazily swirled within the round *ger* like a choking fog. I coughed and coughed. But finally I was able to take small, gasping breaths and, still cupping my hands over nose and mouth, managed to squint through tear-filled eyes.

Two old women, one of them the white-haired Echenkorlo, sat facing me on the opposite side of the fire. Both grinned. They were naked from the waist up, their four limp breasts sagging like the empty bladders of goats. Echenkorlo was laughing at me from behind the small carcass of a weasel-like animal that rested upon her palm. She stroked it with one misshapen finger, and even kissed the whiskered lips stretched in their own frozen grin. Held motionless by this strange sight, I didn't at first notice the other old half-naked woman shuffle toward me on her knees with surprising speed. She grabbed my face between leathery hands and screeched with the triumph of a hawk snatching its prey.

"Echenkorlo! You forgot to speak of her beauty!" Ragged and yellowed fingernails pulled at my braid. "Look at this hair—no finer silk has the Khan." My wrists were ensnared, jerked into the air, and displayed as a prize. "And the hands! Strong. Not too big and not too small." The woman, who stank of blood and urine, buried her face in each of my palms for a moment, murmuring words I couldn't understand. Then, breathing heavily, as if she might fall away into a faint, the old woman drew back, marching her gaze along my arm, my shoulder, my neck, and then my face. A rattling gasp escaped her thin body and she jumped closer. "See how the brow curves like the ram's horns above a thin nose? She is a stubborn one. And look at the eyes!" Her toothless face pressed into mine, a rotting stench clamping shut my nostrils. "Just a glimmer or two of gold. Do they see?" she asked over her shoulder. With her clawed hands gripping my cheeks, I could only roll my eyes toward my grandmother to see her shake her head: "No." As if all the air had been sucked from her, the woman shrank, then shuffled on her knees back behind the fire. My fingers touched the greasy film left upon my skin, and my stomach flipped over. I felt my heart, like that of a scared rabbit, fluttering weakly and rapidly inside me.

Dropping the grinning carcass in her lap, my grandmother suddenly gave the other old woman a shove with both hands. The other woman squealed and shoved back but, after a brief tussle of flailing arms and slapping hands, scrambled aside. Then my grandmother edged over, leaving me the seat of honor facing the door. Both wrinkled faces turned toward me, smiling and nodding eagerly. But as if frozen to the spot, I could only look around me, thinking, What den of danger have I walked into?

My eyes were growing accustomed to the smoke-filled *ger* and they widened in amazement at the clutter. You see, my people take pride in living with few things, carrying only those possessions necessary to survive on the steppe. But Echenkorlo's *ger* was ajumble with curiosities I could not name.

To begin with, the walls were draped with spotted and striped pelts and dark, furry bags of all sizes. I remembered then my mother telling me that Echenkorlo, traveling alone, had visited lands far beyond those of our people. With only her oxcart and a small goat or two, she had traveled north to a place where she said all was white and people harnessed deer to carts with no wheels. And she had traveled south, where she said a quiet people lived all their lives on boats in the water. She even claimed, in crossing a *gobi,* to have spotted Almas, the legendary fur-covered half-man and half-animal, though I smiled inwardly at such silliness.

The hands were still waving at me, urging me to the seat of honor, so, choosing the path closer to my grandmother, I forced my unsteady legs around the fire. I felt the piercing eyes of both old women burning through me with each limping step. Sticky with a nervous sweat, I collapsed cross-legged between them and waited.

From the corner of my eye I saw it coming. The greasy hand of my grandmother's companion flashed across me. Leather strips whipped through the air and I felt my twisted foot burn. At the same instant blue sparks leaped from the fire, layering another cloud of strange perfume in the smoky air. Screaming, I hunched over, covering my head with my arms.

"Udbal! Enough!" My grandmother's sharp voice cut

through the smoke. "All has been tried. We accept the leg." A steaming bowl of tea was thrust into my lap, just below my tucked chin, its hot vapor adding beads of moisture to my already damp brow. Biting my lip and trembling, I timidly tipped my head and looked into my grandmother's face.

It was round and, except for a nubbin of a nose, almost flat. The golden skin must have once stretched across her face as smoothly as water upon a still pond, but now the blazing fire highlighted sagging wrinkles that pulled and rippled around her eyes. I saw reflections of the flames dancing in those gray eyes, sparkling with silent laughter. She was smiling, radiating such warmth that my fear began to melt away.

"We are pleased you have joined us tonight," Echenkorlo said. A slight frown in the direction of her companion brought an additional welcome.

"Yes, we are pleased," the other woman said hastily. Her eyes, half-slitted, still stared at my foot as a cat does a mouse.

Straightening, I took the bowl in my hands and bent my head to sip the tea. My nostrils flared, uncertain of the spicy aroma. Yet my lips sucked in the warm liquid, the musky taste pleasant to my tongue.

"Speak," Echenkorlo commanded.

"This is good tea," I said.

Udbal snickered.

"No." My grandmother drew herself up tall, leaning forward just slightly and concentrating her gaze on my eyes. "Speak of the white mare and the festival."

I felt my face fall. "Oh," I said, sighing, "I see my father told you." I paused, and when no one spoke added, "I made a weak choice."

Both women leaned closer. "How is it weak?" they asked in harmony. "Does she kick?" asked one. "Does she bite?" asked the other. "When you place the saddle upon her back, does she lie down and refuse to run?"

"We can change that, you know," they concluded in unison.

"No, no," I said. "Nothing like that. At least, I don't think so." I sighed again. "The truth is, I haven't even saddled her yet, because she is lame. She limped all the way home from the festival."

Both old women sat back, somehow satisfied. "And why did you—" began Echenkorlo.

"—choose a lame horse?" finished Udbal.

I waited, sipping my tea, letting the fragrant steam tickle my nose. Should I tell them? I wondered. I wanted to tell somebody—I lay awake at nights wanting to tell somebody—but I knew that as soon as I did, it would be shouted that I was "crooked in the head." Then again, my father had already said Echenkorlo's mind was "twisted," so maybe I could risk sharing my secret with these two.

"She spoke to me," I said warily.

The two women leaned forward again, eager, but this time remained silent. All I could hear was the fire crackling and my heart thumping. I continued.

"I was looking over the horses brought for sale or trade. I wanted to find a swift one I could train into a champion for next year's long race. When I got near this white mare I saw she had been kicked by some other horses, and I got off to check her leg and then I . . . thought I . . . heard her say—"

"—help me away from here." Our three voices spoke the words together in an eerie chant.

My tea bowl wobbled. My heart doubled its pounding. "How —how did you know?" I stammered. But then I felt foolish, as if I had been led into a trap. My embarrassment blazed into anger. "Well, if you already knew, then why did you let me tell you?"

"To see if you knew," said Udbal, her lips making chortling sounds deep in her tea bowl. She began noisily blowing bubbles in the brown liquid until she caught sight of my grandmother's narrowed eyes. Just like a child, she blew one last gurgle into her bowl before cradling it in her lap and falling silent. Apparently satisfied, Echenkorlo turned her kind face upon me.

"Why does your choosing of this white mare make you sad?"

The words spilled from my mouth. And my heart. "I wanted to bring home a champion, a horse that would win the most important race next year. And instead I have an old, crippled mare who can hardly walk. I like her, really I do. She's so sweet. But I wanted . . . just once . . . I wanted to bring good luck to my clan." Then, quietly, "I wanted to bring good luck to my father. Now I am always bad luck."

I saw the two old women stare into each other's eyes for several long breaths. Then, as if she had received a wordless message from Udbal, Echenkorlo nodded. Slowly she turned her head toward me.

"You want to ride the race and win. To capture good luck and carry it home. But I ask you, Oyuna, my grandchild, do you not see both good luck and bad luck around you always? Can you not reach out," Echenkorlo said, extending her open palm before me, "and take either good luck or bad luck into your hand?" Her palm turned, closing into a fist upon the empty air. Then she turned her fist back and opened her palm again, this time revealing a tiny amulet carved of black stone. I gasped, surprised. Leaning closer, I saw the small figure of a galloping horse carrying a person upon its back. Before my eyes, gnarled fingers closed, one by one, over the amulet and when they opened once more, Echenkorlo's palm was empty. Udbal giggled.

"Oyuna, my grandchild," Echenkorlo continued, "many years ago the horse crushed your leg. 'Bad luck,' people say. And they pity you. But I say this brought to you good luck. I say that the horse claimed you as its own. That by crushing your leg it freed you from the ground and invited you upon its back to travel with the wind. It is no surprise, then, that the white mare spoke to you."

I sat silent, my jaw still dropping open.

"This white mare has spoken to you," my grandmother continued, "because she knew you would hear her. And you must listen. Do you think, because you walk upon two legs and animals must crawl upon four, that you are smarter or braver?" In the small *ger*'s smoky air, Echenkorlo's round, wrinkled face seemed to float closer. I found myself focusing on a toothless mouth spilling forth wise words. "Every living thing has a talent for which it was created," it said. "And, as you have discovered, Oyuna, every living thing has a voice. Did you not hear the earth spirits within the stream when you thought you were listening to us?" A shiver slithered down my spine. "You must learn to listen with your heart instead of your ears. And see with your mind instead of your eyes, for the water's surface hides the fishes that swim below it."

Echenkorlo sat staring at me, and through me, her eyes looking into mine, smiling. Then she straightened, settled her shoulders back, and said, "Now eat."

Udbal's hand flashed toward the cooking pot, the

gnarled fingers emerging with a chunk of pale meat, which they stuffed into her mouth. Toothless gums chewed and chewed as a brown drool trickled down her chin. Echenkorlo politely nodded toward me. Hesitantly I reached into the pot, found a small piece of meat and, first swallowing hard, fearful of what strange carcass it may have come from, placed it in my mouth. It was mutton! And much tastier than my own bland recipes. Smiling and nodding, I reached in again, but this time Udbal's claws grabbed my hand, holding it over the pot while the meat's juices ran down my wrist. Wide-eyed, I looked over at my grandmother, but although a smile lit her face, her eyes were closed.

Udbal turned my palm upward and pressed her face close to it. A yellowed claw on her other hand drew a trail through the grease, prodded at the fleshy mounds. Then she looked into the fire and for the first time I noticed the shoulder blades of a sheep burning white within the flames. Udbal, grunting, studied the cracks crisscrossing the hot bones.

"Is it so?" spoke my grandmother, opening her eyes.

"It is so." Udbal giggled. "Two lines, two shadows. It is so."

My grandmother spoke in a deep voice, her vacant eyes staring at a place above my head. "Your journey with the white mare is long. Your hands bring change."

I don't know if I truly heard my father calling me then, but, jumping up, I shouted, "Coming, Father!" And, stumbling over legs and pots and pelts and bundles, I shoved my way through the door flap and bolted into the clear, frosty air of night. No indecision in my tracks this time: the cold light of the rising moon showed them heading straight for home.

10. "You Are Chosen!"

1 lay in my bed that night after dinner, eyes still open wide, heart banging. No one knew of my visit. And as I listened to the heavy rhythmic breathing of those sleeping around me—my father, Shuraa, and her two sons; sensible people who would readily laugh at Echenkorlo's strange words—I began to think I was a little crazy for having walked alone into her black *ger.*

The moon that night rose fat and round. The winds had pulled aside the felt collar covering our smoke hole and through this opening poured the moon's brilliance. I watched through drooping eyes as this looping circle of light slipped slowly across my toes, crept up my chest, rested upon my folded hands, illuminating the dirty half-moons of each fingernail, and finally laid its full brilliance upon my face. I closed my eyes to the glare.

Sleep was just pulling its warm blanket over me when, at my elbow, I heard my name whispered: "Oyuna!"

My heart leaped over a beat. I opened my eyes. There,

at the side of my bed, knelt my grandmother, Echenkorlo. Draped across one arm was Bator, purring contentedly.

"Oyuna!" she whispered again. "Did you feel the circle of the moon upon your face? You are chosen. And so you must choose."

I could manage only to stammer, "What? Why . . . did you come here now?"

Following Echenkorlo's gaze to the foot of my bed, I saw, slumping in the moonlight, an old leather pouch. "You will need assistance in the days ahead," she said quietly.

I looked around, wondering why my grandmother's arrival had not awakened anyone else. "I don't understand," I said.

She kept her voice low, speaking so softly that I had to hold my breath to hear her words. "You want to run the race next year and win. To bring good luck. And so you may, my granddaughter, for the white mare has shared a talent with you." She leaned closer. "Never lose her!" Her breath carried the words with a warm rush into my ear.

I exhaled, excitement roaring in my head. Was my grandmother, a shamaness, telling me I would win the race next year? With what horse? I instantly wondered. But again she was whispering, and I had to suck in my breath to listen.

"Now your journey takes you south, where graze ten thousand white mares."

"And one will be mine?" I whispered excitedly. "One will be my swift horse? How will I find her?"

Echenkorlo closed her eyes, clutched Bator to her chest, and rocked back and forth upon her knees. She spoke in a chanting voice. "On the mountains' cold breath fly blackbirds, laying wings of gold at your feet. Fly with them, but follow only your heart."

She opened her eyes and stared at me. I heard her rattly breathing, saw her thin lips flutter. Then, admonishing me sharply to listen, Echenkorlo pressed her face to my ears and whispered for a long time about the many sicknesses and healing of horses. She described herbs and clays and where they could be found, which plants to eat and to avoid, the proper timing for fire and bloodletting. Confusion welled within me, but the urgency in her voice forced me to concentrate. When her learning had filled my ears, my grandmother sat back, silent, and simply stared at me again. After a moment she spoke a few more words.

"Oyuna!" she said softly. "I, too, have felt the pity of others. But always I choose my own path. And I pull my own luck from the air. Remember!"

Now, to tell truth, I cannot remember what happened after this. When next I awakened, the moonlight had left our *ger* and I did not know in that darkness what was real and what was a dream. When I awoke again the sky was just growing pale with the sun's light. Throwing aside the fleece covers, I rushed to look out the door flap.

Echenkorlo's *ger* was gone.

11. The Mountains' Cold Breath

*A*fter Echenkorlo's visit, the moment I opened my eyes each morning, my heart quickened. Is this the day? I wondered. Leaping from bed, I raced into the coldness, searching the pink horizon. But I could see nothing coming. And the winds always whistled and danced around me, brushing first one cheek and then the other, lifting my braid from behind and, when I spun, shoving me with a gust almost to my knees.

In the dark after bedtime, I pulled the old leather pouch, scratched with pictures of strange animals and stamped in brilliant colors, from its hiding place beneath my bed. Night after night I fondled its few prizes: a large, curving fishhook with a line of sinew knotted to it; a short dagger, elegant in its jewel-encrusted handle, deadly in its pointed hardness; a small iron cooking pot, big enough for just one meal of mutton stew; a silver-mounted steel for sparking a fire; three long needles; and one small leather bag, stiff and discolored from much use. As my fingers traced the painted pattern, I wondered who the pouch had belonged to and when I would begin my journey. Echenkorlo had also left me a large packet of herbs, which she had told me to mix with hot water and apply—every other day—in a bandage tied around the injured hind leg of the white mare. On alternate days I was to lead the mare into a deep, cold stream and let her stand while I counted to five hundred.

"But what about the earth spirits?" I had asked, alarmed. "To stand upon them as they travel through the waters is to bring down upon my head the worst of bad luck."

Echenkorlo had only smiled. "First pray for the earth spirits' help in healing your mare," she said, "and the earth spirits will know that you know their power. By asking them to help you with their power, you will not be harmed by them."

And so, though winter blew its bitter fury across the steppes, I regularly sneaked away from camp, leading the white mare. Bowing and praying to the earth spirits, which I could hear gurgling within the ice-covered stream, I begged through chattering teeth that they use their power not to harm me but to heal the leg of my white mare. Then I coaxed the mare onto the frozen surface, the weight of each hoof crashing through the ice and stirring the spirits into a bubbling frenzy. "One-two-three," I began counting, shivering, shifting my weight uneasily from foot to foot and starting at each little noise. I fully expected the gods to pretend not to hear my prayers and to lay me out flat and lifeless in the frozen mud.

Day after wintry day I treated the mare's leg. A hot herb-filled bandage on one day, the cold waters of a stream the next. But after one moon had come and gone, the mare trotted only slightly more steadily and I still dared not climb upon her back. Gradually I stopped the treatments—the day was too cold or I was too tired. And at night I fell into bed, weary but not sleepy, leaving the leather pouch and its contents to gather dust beneath me.

In the cold stiffness of that winter I stopped chasing dreams.

My father's *ger* felt very crowded now that his new wife, Shuraa, and her two sons, eight and twelve years, lived with us. The future promised no better, for she was already full-bellied with my father's child. Shuraa doted on her two boys, never scolding them for tasks poorly done or even left unfinished. She tried to include me in her coddling. Placing her hands on my waist, she would steer me onto a cushion the way one helps an old person with weak bones. Into my hands she would push the easiest of work— sewing or stirring. "So as not to risk further injury to your poor, poor foot," she moaned while my father smiled. My face flushed hot at these times and not from sitting so close to the cooking fire. I know Shuraa fretted and I know she didn't understand, but on more days than not, I fled our *ger:* I simply had to be with the horses.

By winter's end I had fastened a name upon the white mare: Bayan—"rich with beauty and goodness." Or rather, she had fastened the name upon herself. I had tried several other names: Galuut, for she could be as awkward as a goose, and Buran, for she was as white as a blizzard. But at the speaking of each name, the mare had turned her head away from me. At the same time the word *bayan* kept popping into my head. Finally I chuckled and said, "Bayan," and the mare walked right up to me and shoved her soft muzzle against my neck. I threw my arms around her then and felt that all was right with the world. Since the festival at Karakorum I had rarely "heard" Bayan, yet we daily spoke to each other through touch and an exchanging of warm breaths. In moving by her side as she grazed, and listening, I had come to feel a kinship I had never before known. She was my friend.

When my hands ran along her thinning neck, traveled across the gentle slope of her back, I knew in my heart that she was old and that I would never ride her. Perhaps this would be our last season together. All the more reason, I thought, to pass the days at her side watching the clouds tumble across the sky or laughing at the chattering *susliks* popping out of and back into the ground.

Happily, I saw that the fading winter had not been too hard upon Bayan. As the sun shone longer and longer upon the steppes, I watched her move with much less stiffness. Twice, in truth, I saw her gallop out from the herd with barely a hitch in her stride. But other days she rested long upon the ground, still as if carved from white jade, ears pricked eerily toward the horizon. That sight at first gave me chills—Something's coming, I thought— but when my eyes followed, seeing nothing, I decided Bayan's eyes were simply growing cloudy.

For with the melting of the snows, so had melted away my memory of Echenkorlo's visit and her strange words. They were the nonsense of a dream long forgotten, the babble of a child.

Until a blustery morning in early spring when the winds blew strong and straight from the Hentei Mountains in the east.

It was also a blindingly sunny day. Bator and I were warming ourselves on a rock jutting below a hillock, our backs hunched against the wind. I was whistling on a blade of grass cupped between my hands when I saw them coming. Actually it was the horses that saw them first, for in unison they jerked their heads from the sweet grass poking through the snow patches and stared, ears pricked, nostrils flared, into the distance. At their silent alarm, Bator scampered into the tall grasses. I dropped the green blade and scrambled to the hillcrest behind me. Just as quickly I dropped back below the crest, peeking through a wind-whipped thistle bush to watch the strangers approach.

Soldiers! Nearly a hundred mounted soldiers, each carrying a round shield, so that they moved across the steppe as if the great solid walls of Karakorum marched. They were approaching fast, intent, I guessed, on taking our small *ail* by surprise. I had to warn the others! Jumping to my feet, I slid and hopped in a rush down the hillside.

But the dogs in camp had already spotted the strangers and now joined voices in their own yipping alert. As I limped closer to the cluster of *gers* I saw the men of my *ail* gathering the women and young children and shoving them into the small safety of the felt shelters. My eyes and ears were so full of the noisy confusion, I barely noticed the strong grasp of my father's hand upon my arm, steering me forcefully toward our *ger*. With a push I was shoved inside, nearly stumbling over the pile of a wailing Shuraa clutching her two sons onto what little lap her swollen belly allowed.

Against Shuraa's weak cries of protest I turned and crawled back toward the door flap, pushing it out just enough to lay an eye against the slit and watch, panting heavily, what was happening.

The wind blew stronger and stronger, sending young leaves and bits of grass skittering through our camp. It blasted into the approaching line of soldiers, lifting the flaps of their black *dels* up and down like so many birds' wings. The riders had appeared so suddenly, in fact, that it seemed almost as if they had dropped, in one great flock, from the sky. The men and older boys of our *ail* gathered in a small knot at the farthest *ger,* bracing themselves against the wind and waiting. In the next instant the soldiers were upon them, half of the flock settling around the men, spears pointing, holding them helpless. The other half wheeled off toward the horses, waving their arms and shouting wildly.

And then my heart swelled in my throat as I began to understand. The soldiers were after our horses! They must be the Khan's soldiers, then, for I knew that he could take whatever horses he needed from his people. But in my twelve years I had never seen soldiers within our own camp.

Our herd, already nervous with the sudden arrival of the strange men and their horses, flung their tails into the air and took off. I do not like to admit this, but as I watched these soldiers run after our horses, I admired their skills in the saddle. Each rider and his mount worked as one, leaning into the herd and turning the panicked animals this way and that. Shouting and waving their arms, the riders circled the horses, gradually drawing the invisible noose tighter and smaller until the pack came to a stop, confused.

Then, dropping from the sky like a hawk, fell an *urga,* the herdsman's long pole with a leather loop at its end, around the neck of one quivering horse. Exhausted and scared, the horse, a tall, white-nosed bay belonging to an uncle, was dragged from the herd and hobbled. A dozen soldiers moved alongside it to guard against escape. Time after time, I watched the *urga* shoot through the air,

settling around the neck of another of our horses. And I
saw that the soldiers chose only the best. The brief gallop
had proven which of our herd were truly the strongest
and fastest.

Next the noose fell around the head of my father's old
spotted stallion, but a close inspection after pulling him
from the herd caused shaking heads and the *urga*'s release.
After all, even my father and I knew the old stallion had
not many winters left. But one of the young sorrel mares
my father had brought back from Karakorum was taken—
and she with a lovely filly not more than ten days old at
her side!

One by one, horse by horse, the *urga* settled over heads
until thirty of our finest-bred horses stood hobbled apart
from the herd. As the first group grew smaller and the
new group grew larger, frantic neighs filled the air.

And then a horse's familiar scream shot through the
clamor, so shrill that my own scream was drowned. For
out of the herd had lunged Bayan, my white mare, with
the *urga* tightening around her snowy neck. She tore along
magnificently, plunging and bucking, while the rider tried
in vain to bring her to a halt. Just as they entered the
open steppe, another *urga* fell around her head. Restrained
on both sides, Bayan reared and pawed the air. I had never
seen her look so beautiful. Then she ducked her head and
lashed out at one rider with both hind feet. Even at that
great distance I saw the men point and laugh approvingly.
"Spirit!" I heard one shout.

I couldn't believe it—any of it. That my lovely white
mare was no longer lame—that she, my friend, was being
so mistreated—that she was being taken away from me.
"No, no, no!" I screamed over and over far out of earshot
of the soldiers. I watched in helpless horror as the two

riders yanked Bayan toward the smaller herd, while she continued rearing and bucking tirelessly. It took two more men to fit hobbles around her front ankles, and when she knocked one onto his seat with a sharp kick, a back leg was tied snugly to the front pair. I watched through eyes brimming with tears as the soldiers tied more ropes around her, even haltering her to a horse already standing quietly. Bayan finally gave up resisting and stood quivering and nickering fitfully. I saw her looking around and I knew she was searching for me.

I was sobbing now, my shoulders heaving. The scene swam before my tear-filled eyes as in a terrible dream.

Sharp calls were exchanged between the soldiers guarding the men and the ones guarding the horses. Then the first group raised their spears. Swiftly, one after another, with just a threatening point into the chest of a helpless herdsman, new soldiers were added to the Khan's army. I saw three chosen, two uncles and a cousin, who bowed their heads and walked slowly toward their *gers*.

The commander of the soldiers then dismounted and stomped stiffly from *ger* to *ger,* stooping and thrusting his head into each one. When he neared ours, I shrank away from the door flap and sat trembling, trying to stop my crying. And trying to think what I could do to save Bayan.

Shuraa was wailing wildly, clutching her two sons to her and rocking back and forth in a great jumble of flailing hands and legs. I watched numbly as the *tarag* bubbled out of its pot, spilling into the fire and sending up smelly clouds of steam. No one moved to stop it.

A dark head boldly pushed past the door flap, bringing with it a deep voice that bellowed, "Soldiers for the Khan's army!" Wide shoulders followed and soon the large, heavy body of the soldiers' leader swallowed up the remaining space in our *ger*. He carried in with him on his black uniform the pungent odor of sagebrush, of dung smoke and leather oil. When he lifted his head to look around I cringed at the thick, fleshy face, with its single black eyebrow digging a track across a bony brow.

Ignoring Shuraa's arms clasped around her two sons, the man closed his hairy hand around the small wrist of my older stepbrother. In one sharp motion the hand pulled the wrist upward, so that the boy's body had to follow, though it dangled weakly, like a lamb freshly killed for dinner.

"Here is a soldier, I think," the man snarled. "A puny one, but he will do."

"No, no!" screamed Shuraa, jumping to her feet and spilling her younger son off her lap. She propped her short body beneath her dangling son's limp shoulder. "He has a crippled leg—you will see. He can walk no more than a crawl." Thus supporting him, Shuraa bent over and pushed at her son's legs with one hand as if they were the wooden legs of a toy. Curious, the man released his grip. It was then that I saw Shuraa pinch her son, hard, behind the knee. He cried out and limped a painful step forward. "See?" she said, glancing nervously into the hard face of the commander and pulling her son close into her arms. "See? It is my heartbreak to bear, not yours. You do not want a limping soldier."

The man merely glared at Shuraa. His hand reached out and grabbed the boy forward again. The fleshy face was thrust before the boy's wide eyes. "You may limp in the dirt, soldier, but you won't limp in the saddle. Pack your things. Now!" He jerked the boy's wrist to emphasize his point, then, with a cursory glance around the *ger,* one that swept over my head, the large man turned and left. I heard him shout to his men to prepare to leave.

Shuraa was sobbing again in a helpless heap upon the rug, her two sons kneeling, foggy-eyed and unmoving, beside her.

I released in a rush the sobs I had reined in while the terrifying commander was in our *ger*. Head pressed upon my knees, I, too, swayed back and forth, crying out for the lovely white mare that was being taken from me.

I saw something glinting through my tears. Wiping a sleeve across my eyes, I blinked and bent forward. Lying at my feet on the rug was a small gold likeness of a winged horse with a girl on its back carrying flowers in her hands. Instantly I remembered the small black amulet in the palm of my grandmother, Echenkorlo. I reached for the gold figurine, brought it close to my face, and studied the curving form. A loop at the top, molded into the design, told it was an adornment for a belt or a horse's harness.

And then the strangest thing! Holding that winged pendant in my palm, I felt a great calmness settle over me, like the calm that settles just before a storm, giving you a brief moment to prepare for the fury to follow. You scurry around gathering up this, pinning down that, never knowing whether you will even be alive in the morning. Clearly then, as I had at Karakorum, I heard the words in my head: *Now, now, now!* And I knew what to do.

Tightly clutching the gold ornament, I stood and, with the trembling fingers of one hand, quickly unfastened and slipped out of my *del*. One limping step and I was at the side of my older stepbrother, hastily unfastening his dark green *del*. He, too, was trembling, biting his lip and crying. He said nothing as I slipped the *del* from his limp arms and fastened it around my own body. I picked up his orange belt and knotted it around my waist, marking me a boy. Then I dropped the heavy ornament into an inner pocket.

Shuraa suddenly came alive. "No! You can't!" she cried. "You are just a girl. You're weak, crippled."

Wordlessly, but with great assurance, I stepped across her sprawling leg. Shuraa clawed at my hand and shouted, "They're killers, Oyuna! My own father died in the Khan's army. And my first husband. You don't know the danger!"

But there were so many noises buzzing in my head that I could not heed Shuraa. Halting before the cabinet that still held the stuffed doll with one leg dyed red, I stared. The doll leered back, taunting. *Bad luck,* it seemed to whisper through stained lips. Shuraa's words echoed: "You are just a girl. You're weak, crippled." I took a deep breath, picked up the doll, and cautiously laid it facedown. I pulled a knife from the top drawer. Tipping my head to one side, I lifted the knife to my braid and, with a hard sawing motion, cut it off. Then I tucked the knife within my felt boot. From the wall I grabbed my father's fur-trimmed felt hat and pulled it down over my head, nearly hiding my face.

I reached under the bed and pulled out Echenkorlo's dust-covered leather pouch, slinging it across my shoulder. I dipped water into a spare pouch and strapped it around my shoulder as well, then stuffed a handful of dried mutton strips inside my *del.* Lifting my saddle in my arms, I stumbled under all the weight toward the door flap.

Bator was suddenly at my feet, rubbing his body around my legs, eager to follow. He usually trotted out a bit with me when I left on a ride.

"Not this time, Bator," I said, wishing I had a free hand to give him a final pat. "Better you stay inside." He meowed. I didn't look back.

Already the other new soldiers, all relatives of mine, were saddling their horses. Everywhere women were wailing. Not daring to glance to where my father stood, I carried my saddle straight toward the white mare. As I passed beneath the glare of the heavy-browed commander, he noted my limp and grunted, satisfied.

With my heart thumping, I lifted my saddle onto Bayan, the horse I had never ridden. But there was that look in her eye again, the same twinkle promising adventure which I had trusted at Karakorum, and I knew now I was meant to ride her. With the bridle fitted upon her head and the girth tightened around her stomach, I quickly unknotted the hobbles and ropes. Then I stepped into the stirrup, swung my crippled leg over, and sat lightly upon her back. When the soldiers moved to release the hobbles from the horses they were stealing, I was already hidden among the other soldiers riding east. The morning wind blew straight into our faces, chilling our skin with its cold breath. Yet, tucking my face between collar and hat, I smiled. For seated upon Bayan's back I felt as if I had wings.

With a long groan, the white mare plunged to her knees. Like a moonlit wave crashing upon the shore, her belly and hips followed, the thin spray of her tail falling silently at the finish. Her whiteness pooled in the darkness.

"Grandmother!" exclaimed the girl, bolting upright. The old woman reached out to stroke the girl's hair.

Her words were filled with soothing. "All is well," she crooned. "All is well. The time grows near. Here," she said, reaching her hands behind her head, "tie this around her neck." In the girl's palms she placed the pale green pendant carved in the shape of a galloping horse. "It is jade. So that her flanks may loosen and the filly gallop from her as easy as the spring breeze."

Making her way to the mare's side, the girl carefully fastened the pendant's leather thong so that the galloping horse dangled, twirling, just below the white throat. Then she looked at her grandmother. "Why did you say 'filly'?"

The old woman shook her head slightly, nudging the question aside. "Come," she said, motioning with her hands, "there is more to tell."

Reluctant to leave the mare's side, the girl stroked the white mane. "Does it hurt her?" she asked.

Silence answered her words for many moments. "I think," said the old woman, sighing, "she holds within her too much joy to feel pain. Now, come."

When the girl was huddled once again within the thick robes, still warm with the heat of their bodies, the mare lifted her head in their direction. She seemed to be calmly waiting for the story to continue. Relieved, the girl nestled deeper within the warmth and thought about what her grandmother had been telling her.

"Weren't you scared to ride off with all those soldiers?" she asked.

"Yes."

"Where did they take you? Where did you sleep and what did you eat?"

A chuckle rattled the old woman, but her granddaughter wasn't finished.

"Did you never see Bator again? And what about Bayan? Was her leg healed? Did you have to fight anyone?"

Quiet laughter overtook the old woman. "As Tengri sees all, granddaughter, you chatter like the starlings. Now, which do I answer first?"

"Did the soldiers find out you were a girl?"

12. Riding, Riding, Riding

 A journey should begin with the sprinkling of milk upon the horse's head. Sun and stars should light the path, tears and good food welcome the weary traveler. My journey had no such beginning and I knew not its end. I could see neither the land before me nor the land behind me, for black uniforms rode thick on my every side, like the darkest of forests stumping, rootless, across the steppe.

Time that long day was counted out in hoofbeats; when the march rested, by the rhythmic wheezing of the horses. I heard snorts, commands, names of unknown places. The choppy pace would begin again. I rode blindly, bobbing like a twig among trunks in a flooding stream.

I looked up: just a patch of pale sky; still early, the sun warmed my cheeks. Knees banged, swelled purple. Up and down, up and down.

Sometime later the sun warmed my whole head, its heat seeping through the felt hat. Stomach whined. I pushed a dried mutton strip inside my cheek. Let the salt draw water from my mouth, soften it. Chewed, up and down, up and down. When the last bits melted down my throat, still the hooves pounded out a beat.

The sun slid around, warmed my back. The dark forest marched on.

For all my days horseback, I wasn't hardened to such a ride. My thighs burned from bouncing against the wooden saddle. My ankles ached from standing in the stirrups. The bones in my back felt as if they jostled loose from their string and fell, cracking one upon the other, like pebbles tumbling down a dry stream bed.

Only when the sun sank, giving way to darkness, was the command shouted: Stop.

Slowly I unstuck myself from the saddle. Eased an unwilling leg over. But when my feet touched the hard ground, my now-brittle legs nearly shattered with the pain. I fell amid hooves and legs and boots. Fear grabbed me. I found the stirrup with my hand, pulled myself up, only so much clinging baggage. With the colors rushing before my eyes, my fingers unfastened the saddle, managed to slip off the bridle. I fell backward, beneath a heap of wood and leather and wool.

I remember the horses moving away, heads down, pulling at the grass, hearing it rip in their teeth . . . and the soldiers moving away, clustering around fires, murmuring. . . . And I was still slumping, aching, hugging the saddle . . . and letting the tiredness . . . fall over me . . . like a blanket.

13. Welcome Once, Welcome Again

A wetness skimmed my nose. A heavy furriness dropped over my face. In an instant I was awake, blindly pushing at the suffocating weight. When my hands closed around a soft bundle, vibrating with a familiar rumble, my eyes opened wide.

"Bator!" I exclaimed, hugging the little tiger cat to my chest. He shoved his whiskered cheek against mine, kneading my chest in rhythmic affection. Between the purring, Bator's pink tongue fluttered in his gasping mouth. My hands felt his sides heaving in and out. He must have padded behind us all day and night, I thought. And we had come so far! Truly the creature lived up to his name: "Hero."

"You dear little cat-cat," I crooned. Stroking his back with one hand, I pulled at a forepaw with the other. When my thumb pushed aside the short, muddied hairs, I caught just a glimpse of bloody pink leather before Bator, hissing, leaped off my chest. Tail whipping angrily, he stayed just out of arm's reach. Green-yellow eyes glared.

"I'm sorry," I whispered. "Come over." I wiggled my fingers toward the cat's chin. It was Bator's weakness, and with casual feline forgiveness he took a painful step closer and pushed his head into my hand for a scratch. "Your poor, poor feet," I murmured.

It was in stretching my arm toward the panting cat that I realized my own body was hurting. Because I had fallen asleep, exhausted, upon the spot where I had unsaddled Bayan, I had not had a fire's breath to keep me warm. Only the saddle, turned up against the wind, and the saddle rug, stiff with dried sweat, had protected me from the night's cold. The icy chill of the hard ground had been seeping through my body all night, silently stiffening my muscles, freezing my joints. Now I discovered that I had to think very hard about wiggling my toes, for at first I could not feel them within my felt boots. I bent first one knee and then the other as ice crystals shattered, breaking away from my hardened trousers. The warmth that began flowing back to my fingers and toes carried with it sharp pain and I sat up suddenly, hugging my knees to my chest and rocking back and forth, biting my lip to keep from crying out.

Where was I?

I crouched low and took a cautious look around. From out of the drifting fog stepped a bustard. The huge gray and brown bird stopped still, tipping a suspicious orange eye toward me. Then, with an urgent call, she, too, crouched to the ground, tail feathers fanned wide. Five tiny chicks scurried from the grass, across her tail, and up her back. Beating her wings, the mother bustard flew her children to safety.

Loneliness pressed doubly hard upon me. My eyes scanned the sparse grassland stretching in all directions. It looked exactly like the valley in which I had awakened yesterday, except that this stone-colored sky sheltered no familiar cluster of white *gers*. Instead, a half-dozen bounds from my side, in pile after dark pile, slept the Khan's soldiers. They had lined their upturned saddles against the steppe's cold blasts and now lay in heaps between these windbreaks and the dead embers of last night's fires. Lifting my gaze past them, I saw that the distant horizon was just beginning to glow copper, tingeing a line of heavily padded clouds. A biting wind came rushing along the ground, slapping into my side and ruffling Bator's fur. The muffled crunching of frozen grasses told that the horses grazed somewhere far behind me, but my neck was too stiff for me to turn and look.

Bator climbed into my lap and began pushing his way, nose first, inside my *del*. At first I thought he was trying to get warmer, but then I realized that he was probably smelling the mutton strips I had carried yesterday.

"I'm sorry, Bator," I said, pulling the eager cat away. "They're all gone." Persistent, he kept butting his head against my *del*. "There's nothing in there for you," I said sadly, tugging at him again. Bator jumped from my lap, stalked a few steps, and sat down, glaring at me once more. Then he abruptly rose and, tail rigid in the air, trotted into the grass. "Bator!" I called softly, not wanting to alert the soldiers. "Come back! We can find something." But the grasses remained still. I sank my head upon my knees, biting my lip.

What had I done?

My hand traveled along my *del,* feeling for the gold ornament hidden in its inside pocket. Fingers closed around its comforting weight. "Wings of gold," my grandmother had said. She had been right: I had flown with them. But to where?

I closed my eyes, thinking back to that dreamlike night in my *ger*. What else had she said? Something about a place with ten thousand white mares. That's where I would find my swift horse. No matter how scared I was, or how dangerous the journey—no matter who tried to stop me—I had to find my swift horse before I could return home. And I had to stay with Bayan. "Never lose her!" I heard the warm breath of Echenkorlo's words in my ear as if she knelt beside me.

I knew I had to get to Bayan. I had to be the first to saddle her. Never would anyone else ride her. Stiffly unfolding my arms and legs and rising, limping, to my feet, I gathered the saddle and bridle and crackling blanket and set off for the herd.

The cold copper sun was just clearing the horizon when I reached the horses, my sides panting like Bator's. I could hear some of the soldiers now tromping behind. Even among the hundreds of other horses, Bayan's milky hide was easy to spot. I picked my way through the herd, most of whom had been hobbled by their more responsible riders. I was lucky that Bayan had chosen to stay with the herd the past night, rather than gallop where she pleased.

When I pushed my way beneath the neck of the last horse, my heart nearly stopped. Bayan stood, grazing, on only three legs. Her other leg, the far hind one, was hitched up, with just the toe resting upon the ground. I dropped the tack in a heap and bent to place my hands upon her leg, fearful of swelling. Bayan snorted in alarm. Before I could look, a powerful hand gripped my shoulder and spun me around.

"You one-legged half-wit! What are you doing?"

I looked up into the fleshy face of the commander who

had shoved his way into our *ger* yesterday morning. So
hard was I trembling in his iron grip that I couldn't speak.

"Are you deaf as well?" he roared. "What are you
doing?"

I swallowed. "Saddling my horse," I croaked.

"Who gave you an order to saddle?" He shook me as
if I were a felt doll.

"No one," I whispered.

With a hard shove, the commander pushed me onto the
ground. Bayan snorted again and sidestepped, lifting her
hooves clear of me. "You are to wait for my order to
saddle," the man continued to shout. "Do these words
reach your ears, you skinny son of a sheepherder?" Reaching down, he pinched my ear between his thick, calloused
fingers. I yelped. "You are to wait for my order to saddle,
for my order to eat, for my order to sleep!" The commander's voice rose with his temper. I felt the blood drain from
my face. He let go of my ear. Bending far over, he pressed
his smelly face next to mine and shouted, "Do you understand me?"

Holding my breath, eyes nearly closed in terror, I nodded. Through my squinting view I saw a mass of splotched
and pockmarked skin dotted with black pimples. Scraggly
dark hairs sprouted from a dirty chin. The night black
eyes rolled, storming, in yellow seas. Pushed so close to
the man's face, I could even see the target of his eye, the
darkest part, swelling like an angry black moon. I watched
the crusted eyelid drop and rise. Watched the moon shrink
and puff up again. The commander blinked, muttered
something under his rancid breath, and blinked again.

In a flash, his heavy arm knocked the fur-lined cap from
my head. "Koke Mongke Tengri!" he exclaimed, hailing
the great blue sky spirit. "You're a girl!"

Speechless with fear, I just trembled.

For a moment the surprise held the commander speechless as well. But too soon his resurging anger swept away the silence. "What are you doing out here?" he bellowed. "The Khan's army is no place for a girl. Why aren't you stirring *ayrag* beside your husband's fire?"

Timidly, chin tucked, I responded, "I have no husband."

"Then why are you not helping your mother?"

"I have no mother."

"Koke Mongke Tengri!" he exclaimed again, shaking his head. The commander rose to his feet and ordered me to get up as well. "I repeat my question. What are you doing out here? Why have you disguised yourself as a soldier? And look at me when you answer or I'll have you skinned upon this spot!"

Raising my quivering chin, I managed to look into the commander's stormy face and answer. "You stole my mare," I said. "I am staying with her."

"Stole your mare?" Spittle splashed my face. "You have no mares—no sheeps, no goats, no clothes upon your back." The furious man grabbed the short collar of my *del* as if he would rip it from my body. "Each of these things—everything—belongs to the great ruler, Kublai Khan. He takes what is his when he needs it. And now his army, this army, needs horses. So we take what belongs to the Khan."

"Then you have to take me, too." I heard these calm words come from my mouth at the same time I felt my knees would collapse from trembling.

The commander only grew more angry. "You prove yourself the half-witted son—er, daughter," he sneered, "of a sheepherder, for already I have told you that no girl is going to ride with this army."

"I go with my mare."

"You will go where I say!"

We both saw the other soldiers approaching cautiously now, carrying their saddles and waiting for orders. The commander seemed flustered. He lowered his voice, though not his anger. His words were threatening. "You will go where I say, and when I say. And I am saying that you will walk straight inside the first *ger* we come upon and not show your face until this army rides over the horizon. I choose not to separate your head from your neck at this instant only because I have three daughters of my own and know their foolishness. But if you so much as say another word—just one word—you will be dropped—with no horse and no head—wherever your words fall. Do you understand me? A nod will do."

I nodded.

"Now, place your saddle upon another horse. Only a fool rides the same animal two days together. And wait for my command to step up." He spun around and stomped off.

I nearly fell to the ground again, so badly was I shaking. I heard Bayan nicker behind me and then she was at my side, rubbing her head vigorously against my shoulder. I happily saw that she wasn't lame after all, but stood squarely on all four legs. Just to be sure, I ran my hands up and down her furry legs, but each was cool and hard— no swelling! Patting her on the rump, I picked up my father's hat and pulled it down upon my head.

Then I looked around for another horse to saddle. The young sorrel mare that my father had bought at Kara-korum, the one with the days-old filly at her side, was grazing just a few horses away. Since she was familiar to me, I pushed my way through the herd and fit the bridle over her head. She did not resist my placing the saddle upon her back and continued grazing contentedly. As I bent to tighten the girth around the mare's still-fat belly, I heard a muffled yet urgent mewing coming from behind and glanced over my shoulder to see Bator marching straight toward me. Head held high, ears pinned back in determination, he dragged the limp body of a fat *suslik* between his legs. For the second time that morning I pulled the cat to me and hugged him.

Bator's squelched cry made two soldiers nearby look over their saddles with curiosity. Turning my back to them, I quickly scooped up the dead *suslik* and stuffed it inside my *del*. I stuffed Bator in after it. Then I quickly mounted the sorrel mare, remembered the commander's threats, and stepped down, all the while hoping no one noticed the two lumps, one squirming, that bulged beneath my *del*.

Holding the reins, I stood close to the mare's neck, watched the filly suckle, and waited. The commander rode by. I felt his hot glare upon my back but I didn't turn around. At last the order to mount was given. With a great creaking of leather, the hundred-plus soldiers stepped into their saddles, I among them. Then we sat, waiting, as the commander rode up and down, pushing the men into groups of ten. Each group had its own leader, although the hot-tempered man who knew my secret commanded everyone. When he rode past me again, I hunched over, trying to look as timid as possible.

"You ride in the ninth *arban*, just in front of the horses," he shouted, pointing to me. Looking straight ahead, he rode on as I reined the sorrel toward the herd, the filly trotting at our side.

The ninth *arban*—a good sign, I thought. I kept my face shielded as I rode past the *arbans* holding the other members of my *ail*. I hoped they believed me to be my stepbrother. All knew him to be shy, always sidling away from attempts at conversation. Surely no one would choose this moment to call out.

Excitement was springing up within me. I was still with Bayan. I had Bator back. I had dinner lying warm on the outside of my belly, and it would be inside later. And nine was a lucky number. How hard could it be to find my swift horse and return home, triumphant?

I laid my free hand on the pocket holding the flying horse figurine that had started this adventure. I began to believe that my luck had changed. That the good luck brought by the ornament was outweighing the bad luck I carried in my leg. And on that cold spring morning, far away from my home, surrounded by strangers who cared not for me, I sighed happily.

14. The Luck That Lurks upon the Steppe

With the order to ride, a thousand hooves stamped the frozen ground. Bator had stopped squirming. I imagined he slept, hoped he wasn't gnawing the *suslik*. Wrinkling my lip, I thought about bouncing along the whole day with blood and guts squishing inside my *del*.

The morning's pace was not as fast as before. I guessed the commander had wanted to put a safe distance between his newly captive soldiers and their *ail*. But he had no need to worry about me. My heart already skipped ahead of the horses.

Now, you will ask me, didn't I miss my father? And I answer honestly: yes. But our ties had begun to loosen on the night he gave me the silver earrings—the price that would send me from our *ger*. It was right that I should leave. And the winged gold ornament had shown me the way.

Throughout the day the scowling commander galloped back and forth, scrutinizing his groups of soldiers. Riding in the *arban* just ahead of the extra horses, I was able to look over my shoulder frequently to check on Bayan. To my eyes she traveled easily, neck stretched level in an easy, swaying trot. Some of the other horses, ones ridden especially hard the previous day, moved more slowly and the soldiers riding at the back had to beat them with sticks to push them up with the herd. My heart cried out when I saw one old liver-colored gelding, nostrils fluttering, finally hunch under the blows of the sticks and refuse to go on. With loud curses, the soldiers passed around him, closed up the caravan, and left the gelding to drift alone.

The odd thing about the days I rode as a soldier was the steppe. Always I had known the grasses to quiver with wildlife, but that spring they stood still, eerily empty. Each afternoon, the commander sent out hunting parties to bring back game, but time and again they returned empty-handed, shrugging their shoulders and muttering about bad fortune. The hungry soldiers began to grumble. When the dried meats and powdered mare's milk they carried were gone, they took knives and—to my horror— slashed the necks of the very horses they were riding! I had to turn my head from the sight of their greedy lips sucking the oozing blood. With the wipe of a sleeve across a satisfied mouth and a grimy hand pressed briefly against the wound, a soldier would coolly pull himself back into the saddle and kick his meal and his mount forward.

One gray morning we spotted a herd of *saiga* scattered across a far hillside and a cheer rippled among the men. The commander quickly held the *arbans* noiseless behind his upraised arm while a hunting party sneaked up on the herd. Suddenly, without letting fly a single arrow, they turned and galloped back. Ashen-faced, the hunters kept looking over their shoulders and nervously flicking their fingers toward the earth and sky. When we moved on, I saw why.

The herd of *saiga* we had spotted was actually a herd of long-dead carcasses, the hollow remains of a thousand creatures that had starved to death in the past winter. No one spoke a word as we steered our horses in a wide arc around the withered bodies, only a few of which had been gnawed upon by predators. Certain that the bad luck of the dead, so widespread here, would pounce at any moment, I gripped the gold ornament within my pocket until my own nails drew blood from my palm. The soldiers that yet had mare's milk flung drops into the sky and upon the earth.

The instant the last *arban* cleared the silent herd the commander gave the order to gallop. And gallop we did. Thumping our horses' sides with our heels, we raced in a frenzy to gain the next hill. And the next and the next. With fear birthing confusion, the *arbans* frayed, jumbling one into the other. Even some of the spare horses struck out on their own, pushing past the ones carrying riders. You can imagine my surprise when Bayan's white nose pulled alongside my knee. Ears pinned, eyes blackened, the mare hurtled past. Her hooves ripped the soil as she caught the rider ahead of me, steadily bested him, then targeted the next horse and rider. Heads turned to watch and pride, swirling with wonder, rose within me. Just as Bayan's white body began bumping with those of the lead horses the commander called us to a halt. Jerking his horse's mouth, he trotted up and down, shoving his soldiers back into their proper *arbans* and ordering that the spare horses be gathered as well. When Bayan was trotted past me I could see that her sides were heaving and that her nostrils flared red. But I swear to Tengri that at that moment she tipped her head and winked.

So many questions in my head then! Could Bayan really race? She had been challenging the front-runners, hadn't she? But I thought she was too old. And, if no longer lame, at least not sound enough to gallop a festival race that pounded a horse's legs half the morning prior to reaching the finish line.

Before my mind stopped spinning and even before the mounts stopped blowing, the commander ordered us all into a strong trot. The tired horses leaned into their work less enthusiastically now but their riders, including myself, urged them forward with hands and heels. We were so itchy to escape this lifeless, eerie spot on the steppe into which we had fallen that we rode well into the night, and arose in the still-dark to hurry on.

The light that finally touched the empty grasses that next morning came from a pale sun veiled by a cold haze. With unexplained suddenness, a bone-dry wind kicked up, gusting so hard that the horses had to bend their heads and push into it with their shoulders. Thick manes and tails whipped crazily. *Dels* flapped; hats blew off. My eyes were tearing so badly that I yanked my father's big hat low over my brow, preferring to squint through its fringe of wolf hairs. The blustery cold pierced even the fleece-lined *del* of my stepbrother, and I was grateful for Bator's lumpy warmth against my stomach.

Midday—with the wicked wind yet blowing furiously— we came upon a shallow pond. The commander called for a halt that the horses might drink and rest. Usually the soldiers and I dismounted to stretch our legs and rest as well, but this day we remained huddled in our saddles, too numb to move. I fed out the reins so that the horse I was riding, a mealy-colored mare with faint brown stripes on her legs, could lower her head to the water. Pushed by the strong wind, crescents of white scooted across the surface, splashing waves upon the horses' hooves. The mealy mare snorted suddenly and jumped sideways, nearly dumping me. Looking at the spot where she had just been standing, I saw a shimmering silver and black fish flopping upon the muddy bank. A strong murmur, like one of the waves, was rolling among the other riders and, when I lifted my head, I saw that all along the pond's edge, the wind was lifting the very fish from the water and tossing them upon the bank. Silver bodies arched and leaped, slapping helplessly against the mud. Some flopped all the way into the blowing grasses of the steppe and disappeared from sight.

When the murmur reached my ears, I heard the words "bad luck" over and over. It was an evil sign that fish tried to swim upon the land, the men were saying. Perhaps this was not so much a bad area of the steppe as that something bad was riding among them. Soon the attention focused on the members of my *ail,* for we were the newest soldiers, and it was whispered that one of us carried the bad luck. My pulse raced. I hunched over, trying to sit very small and unnoticed upon the back of the mealy mare.

The commander came riding along the muddy bank, his black horse prancing and snorting against the wind and a tight rein. Irritated, the man shouted a sharp command to move on. The soldiers began clustering in their groups of ten. I likewise reined my horse toward the line, but as the commander passed me he leaned forward and glared.

"What are you hiding?" he said, pointing at my bulging *del.*

Pretending not to hear him, I kicked the mare and hurried forward to join my assigned *arban.* But the commander surged alongside, shoving his horse's shoulder against the mare to stop her.

"You must truly be deaf as well as crippled," he sneered. "Do you not hear me?"

Scared sick, I answered in a small voice. "It's my cat," I said.

"What?" he yelled. "Did you say a cat? A cat! Koke Mongke Tengri! A cat!" He slapped his forehead in the manner of my father's exasperation and the shadow of a smile flitted across my face. "Koke Mongke Tengri!" he went on. "First a cripple—who becomes a girl—who hides a cat! I should never have stopped at your puny *ail*. What made me stop there? And why did I choose that crazy white mare that has seen too many winters?" He thrust out his jaw, squinting his yellowish eyes at me. "What is it about this one mare that a girl gathers her cat and follows it through this miserable weather? Tell me!"

I had little to lose, I thought. My life already rested in the hands of this ugly man. So, facing him, I said simply, "She speaks to me."

"She! Koke Mongke Tengri, you are half-witted!" He began to rein his horse away when I saw a look of near fear come over him. "Or are you some sort of shamaness?" His eyes traveled quickly over my clothing, my leather pouch, my hands. "Can you change the weather? Is it you who has caused the fish to swim upon the land?" Not waiting for an answer, the man shook his head and said, "I had not seen weather this foul until we visited your *ail*." He muttered some words I couldn't hear, words that ended with "my ornament of luck." Pounding his heels into his horse's sides, the commander galloped to the head of the line. But not before the wind carried his last words into my ears: "Everything has gone wrong since that ornament dropped from my side."

At that moment I felt the gold ornament weigh heavily inside my pocket. It was true, then! The flying horse did bring good luck, and now I carried it! An uneasiness in my stomach told me I should return it, but as I let my wind-reddened hand fall across the pocket, patting it protectively, I knew I would never release it from my side. Reaching inside my *del*, I patted Bator's head. He shoved his wet nose against my fingers. Moving my hand past him, I also felt the hardened body of another *suslik* that he had hunted. Bator and I would eat meat again tonight.

With the sinking of the pale sun, the gusting faded. The silence, after so much deafening wind, felt doubly eerie and again no one spoke as we rode north. Throats painfully dry, hands and faces cracked, we finally stopped for the night.

I had taken to sleeping apart from the others, beside my own small fire, and this bothered no one. Although I suffered more of the night's cold, I avoided recognition. That evening the distance allowed me to hold the skinned *suslik* on a stick over the embers while a great number of the soldiers held only bowls of weak tea. Bator huddled within the shelter of my upturned saddle, green eyes shining as he watched the *suslik* blacken.

I was worrying that evening about Echenkorlo's warning to me: "Follow only your heart . . . choose your own path." We had been traveling east, but this day we had turned north. I would not find my swift horse there, I knew, if in fact I was still to find one. I did not yet know if Bayan was sound enough for the long race. Her sprint yesterday had brought on no lameness today. But the lure of ten thousand white mares made me want to search farther. And so, after gnawing the meat from the *suslik*'s bones, I tossed anxiously upon the ground, my heart tugging in one direction, the Khan's commander forcing me another.

The sun shone bright and clear the next morning,

warming the spirits of horse and human alike. Bayan would be somewhat rested by now and I had decided even before I stirred from beneath the saddle blanket that I would ride her that day, testing her stamina.

But as I walked toward the herd carrying my saddle, I saw that another soldier was already trying to force his bit into her mouth. Bayan was fighting him, tossing her head out of reach. The soldier booted her in the stomach. The sound of bone cracking upon bone split the air as Bayan's jaw swung hard against the soldier's face. In instant and fierce response, the soldier's fist flew through the air, punching her tender muzzle. Before his fist returned to his side, I was shoving my small body between him and Bayan.

"Stop!" I cried. Without a glance, the soldier shoved me to the ground and threw the bridle around Bayan's head again, banging the metal bit against her clenched teeth.

Now, in my homeland, wrestling is an art, an admired skill that every boy masters. I had no such training and so cannot say if my next move was truly skillful. But it worked. Crouching, I threw all my weight against the soldier's legs, low and hard, so that, with a surprised grunt, he toppled to the ground. Bayan trotted away. Which left me alone—and eye to eye with a furiously growling man twice my size. My scrambling escape backward was stopped short by a wall of tall, rigid boots.

"What is happening here?" Immediately I recognized the bellowing voice as that of the commander. I leaped to my feet along with the angry soldier. He was spluttering.

"This skinny little—" he began ranting, but the commander cut him off.

"Silence!" he shouted. "You will save your fighting for

the enemy. Now, each of you, choose other horses and saddle them before I—"

"Commander!" a voice called from afar. "Commander!" Heads turned to see a young man in a badly torn brown *del* limping toward us. He led a well-muscled bay with a white blaze, three white socks, and, quite apparently, a painful limp as well. Twin goatskin bags were slung across his back. It took the pair several moments to reach us, in which time the angry soldier slipped off to saddle another horse and I stubbornly moved toward Bayan. She moved toward me, too, so I was able to listen to the young man's words while I fitted my saddle upon her back.

"Commander," he said when he reached the soldiers' leader. "I am an arrow rider for Kublai Khan, delivering to him a great prize. My horse slipped on a shale slope beyond that hill and I fear we both suffer broken bones." I could see now that the young man hitched one shoulder higher than the other and cradled his arm motionlessly against his side. "I ask you in the name of the Khan to send your best horse and rider in my place, at least to the next arrow station."

"How far is the next station?" the commander asked.

"No more than a day's ride—straight toward that notch in the Hentei Mountains." The arrow rider moved his chin gently southward, in the direction of the horizon's blue mountains.

"I'll go," offered a tall, swaggering soldier, leading his underfed horse to the commander's side.

The commander gave him no answer. "Give me the *paiza* and the message," he ordered the young man.

The arrow rider untied a thick gold medallion the size of a man's hand that hung from a rope around his waist, as well as a small leather pouch on another rope hidden

inside his clothing. At once the commander walked the
few steps to where I stood beside the saddled and bridled
Bayan and, feeding the smaller rope through the opening
of my *del*, secured the pouch against my bare stomach.
Then he roughly fastened the gold medallion around my
waist.

"Huh?" exclaimed the swaggering soldier.

"Commander, are you certain that—" the injured arrow
rider began.

"This mare can run," he said crisply, "and this one can
ride her like no one else. Besides, sending them off will
solve both our troubles."

As he doubled the knot, the commander's hairy hand
brushed the solid weight hidden within my pocket. "What
is this?" he muttered, boldly reaching inside to pull the
gold ornament into the light. "Why, it is mine!" he cried.
"You stole it from me!"

"No!" I said, shaking my head vigorously. "I found
it—on the floor of my *ger*."

"Then why did you not return it to me?"

I wasn't sure how to answer, for he was right. But,
gazing longingly at the winged gold horse in his palm, I
just had to whisper, "Is it true it brings luck to its owner?"

A queer sort of look churned in the dark eyes of the
commander. He shoved his gold ornament back inside my
pocket, jerked the goatskin bags from the injured bay, and
threw them across Bayan's saddle. With the briefest of
glances into my face, he said, "Deliver this valuable, then
let the luck of that winged horse carry you home. Your
father misses you." Clamping a rough hand upon my
shoulder, the man all but lifted me into the saddle. He
slapped Bayan upon the rump, making her jump forward,
but I reined her to a quick halt.

Leaning down to the commander's ear, I whispered again. "But I can't go yet. My cat—"

Fury boiled up inside the man, bursting forth in the kick of his boot into Bayan's tail. She pinned her ears and bucked.

"Commander," the arrow rider was saying nervously, "it appears this rider is unfit. I'm certain you realize that not to deliver the Khan's desire—and swiftly—is death! Perhaps you have another . . ." His voice trailed off.

The commander had rushed to my leg, jerking the reins so hard that Bayan's mouth gaped sideways in pain. "Ride! Now!" he roared. "You ride for those mountains and don't look back or, as Tengri watches all, I'll have the hides of you and your mare!" Flinging free the reins, he booted Bayan again. This time I bent over her neck and, gulping, sent her galloping as fast as she could.

15. Wolves in the Water

The hot stares of the soldiers pricked my back like arrows. I ached to wait for Bator, but the harsh words of the injured rider swirled within my ears as I galloped: "Not to deliver the Khan's desire—and swiftly—is death!"

Bayan was slowing, gathering her body to slide down a pebbly embankment, when a needle-sharp pain stung my thigh. An arrow! I thought. Someone is firing upon us! My hand felt for blood, found fur. Glancing down I saw Bator clinging wild-eyed to my trouser leg, his back legs kicking the air. I yanked him by the scruff of his neck into my lap. One hand pressed upon him firmly as I bent again over Bayan's neck and shouted for her very best. I prayed for her weak leg to hold strong.

Only when we had put a great distance between ourselves and the Khan's soldiers did I rein the old mare to an easier pace. The two-beat trot felt slightly unsteady and I noticed the white head bobbing with each stride—

not good signs. Worried, I pulled Bayan to a walk. As she caught her breath, my eyes searched the mountainous horizon for the guiding notch. There it was—a little east and south: I was back on the track to a horse both strong and swift!

But it seemed that day that the gods decided to test my desire.

Late in the morning black clouds rolled in to dump bag after bag of hard rain upon our heads. Bayan had to pick her way carefully, for the steppe turned greasy with mud. Soon so much water floated upon the land that it seemed as if we walked on an endless lake. Lifting my head, I groaned. The notch in the mountains had disappeared.

The storm swept past, but low clouds and a raw wind took its place. Cold, wet, and shivering, we hunched our shoulders and tried to follow a stream toward the mountains, though foaming brown waters spilled over its banks, blurring the true course. Bayan bravely splashed through the floodwaters, steadily plunging ahead.

When at last a brilliant sun blinked between fleeing clouds, it shone upon towering mountains that seemed to have risen up suddenly right before our faces. Bayan halted and stamped a hoof impatiently: Which way?

Sagging in the saddle, drenched to the bone, I tiredly looked around. The mountains rose so closely that I could not see to their tops. Water flowed everywhere; we were hopelessly lost. The soldiers had been right, I thought. Bad luck had been riding with them. By casting me out they had unknowingly freed themselves. But it seemed that bad luck would always ride with me, clamped to my side, forever and always.

Or would it? Pushing numb fingers inside my soggy *del,* I found the gold ornament and lifted it into my palm.

Closing my eyes and wishing very hard to be led to the arrow station, I prodded Bayan's sides. She stepped uncertainly at first, then abruptly leaned forward, lunging headlong into a loud-splashing, ground-covering gallop.

I opened my eyes—and screamed! Loping at my left heel, red tongue flopping, was a wolf! The journey was over. We were dead. Squeezing shut my eyes, I waited for the sharp-fanged leap.

But it never came. Squinting through half-parted lids, I looked again. Now there were three wolves! And another was splashing across the steppe. Yet the yellow-eyed creatures didn't turn upon us. And Bayan seemed to be running with them rather than from them.

Suddenly I remembered the silvery wolf that had crossed our path on the way to Karakorum, bringing luck to our journey. Were these wolves bringing luck now? Were these hunters actually guiding us?

The floodwaters shimmered a fiery orange as the sun began sinking. We galloped into a stand of tall trees and Bayan's hoofbeats became muffled by mud and fallen leaves. Oddly, I thought I heard music far ahead. I reined her to a walk to listen. For some reason, Bator chose that moment to scramble from my *del* and jump to the ground. When I looked down, both Bator and the wolves were gone.

"Where did the wolves go?"

"I don't know. To smoke in the air, a shadow beneath a tree."

"What was the music?"

Smiling, the old woman rested against the stable wall and sighed.

"The *morinkhour*," she said, "the horse harmony. I don't believe you have this instrument in your country. But then you couldn't, for it was born of our people's love of the horse. It is told that long, long ago, a nobleman had a favorite horse who died. So heartbroken was he that he pulled hairs from his horse's tail for the strings and for a bow. And from the very best wood he fashioned the *morinkhour,* carving a likeness of his horse's head at the top of the instrument. When this nobleman drew the bow across the strings, he heard in their music the tremulous whinnies of his horse. He recognized the burbling of the many streams they had splashed through and the humming of the winds that had shared their travels. In this way he would always remember his finest friend."

The round-sided mare, restlessly circling the stall again, paused to swing her head up and down and nicker emphatically, bringing smiles to the two humans in the corner. The girl asked another question.

"Where was the music coming from?"

"From the arrow station. The wolves had led us there. It was headed by a woman as strange as she was large, a woman who, I believe, both loved me and hated me."

16. The Fat Woman with the Fast Horses

She was the fattest woman I had ever seen, the one who pushed her head through the door flap long into that afternoon.

I met her raised eyebrows with a teeth-chattering greeting. *"Sain bainu?"* I said. How do you do?

"My, my, my," she stammered as her bulk filled the entrance. She clucked her tongue in the same way my mother had. "I did not hear your bells, young man. You and your horse tippy-toed up to my door quiet as a couple of foxes." Her mountainous shoulders scraped the narrow door frame and for a moment I feared she might step forward, carrying the whole station upon her back. But, grunting like an ox, she managed to shift her weight around, lift her chin from soft necklaces of fat, and call, "Delger! An arrow rider! Bring round the bay."

Waves of silk stained a ripe berry color rustled with her turning. I noticed the fine embroidery and wondered how many days it had taken some poor hunched-over girl to stitch all that material. Pale coral earrings, carved in an openwork design and much too fine for everyday wear, brushed the woman's sloping shoulders. Just as my eyes were traveling down to the brightly sewn coverings worn on feet that, surprisingly, were little bigger than mine, she turned back to me. I hid my interest in her elaborate attire and, untying the heavy gold medallion engraved with writing from my waist, leaned over to hand it to her. I watched the plump eyelids flutter upward in amazement.

"A messenger of the Khan himself!" Her lips tasted the words with obvious pleasure. Then the small brown eyes shot back to me and I ducked my chin within its surrounding collar, hoping to protect my identity. She thought she had embarrassed me.

"Forgive me, young man!" The woman was swaying from foot to foot like an overgrown girl and grinning. "Understand you are a surprise to us. The Khan's arrow riders rarely ride out this far. Mostly we just see herdsmen riding for a shaman or soldiers sending for supplies or two tribes announcing a marriage." At that moment a broad-chested boy led a red bay horse, bridled and saddled, around the corner. Bayan nickered and the bay answered. Without pause, the woman continued, "And a marriage announcement is just the message I'd like to receive, yes, Delger?" The boy rolled his eyes. Handing his mother the reins, he silently turned to check the saddle's fastenings.

Chuckling, the woman swatted her son's back with a bearlike paw. Then she returned the medallion to me and began giving directions to the next arrow station. "Now," she said, "notice that path over there beside the stream? Follow it through the thicket and up the mountain until you see—here!" She was slapping the reins against my thigh. "Hop off! The Khan's things must not be delayed. And while this bay may look small he'll carry you swift as a river and just as smooth as if you floated on it. Now, when you get to the clearing . . ."

My ears no longer followed her directions, for I suddenly understood that she wanted me to leave Bayan and ride on with her horse. Panic-stricken, with my pounding heart drowning out her words, I watched the woman waggle a fat finger in the direction of the thicket. No, I thought. I can't leave Bayan. No.

"No!" the woman said abruptly, clapping her hands together. "Although that gold *paiza* of the Khan shines like the sun, it can't light the darkness, now can it?" Turning, she began impatiently slapping the reins against her son's arm. Still without speaking, he took them and shouldered the bay aside.

"You rest here tonight, young man," the woman ordered. Tipping her weight precariously forward, she squinted. Eyes hunkering behind folds of flesh examined Bayan's legs. "By the looks of your mare, she could use a rest as well. A bit old for such hard riding, isn't she?" The woman, breathing heavily, twisted her head up toward me. "Has the Khan fallen on such hard times that he employs the likes of her for his fastest?" Beads of sweat popped out upon her forehead as she straightened. Labored panting nearly choked her chuckles. "You tell the Khan when you get back to him to come see me—Genma. Tell him I have the finest, fastest horses in all his lands. Tell him," she said, winking, "that I will back any of my horses in a race against any of his." She clapped her hands again. The sharp noise jumped into the long shadows, disappearing into the depths of the forest. A cold wind lunged out to bite at my back.

And suddenly I wanted nothing more than to step out of my saddle and sit beside a cheery fire with friendly people. And to listen to tales of fast horses.

"Now, come," she was saying, slapping my knee. "Step down. Your mare will be well tended by my son. Do you like marmot? I have two fat ones cooking in a pot on the fire right now. And as fast as my horses are, even better is my cooking. Hah!" she laughed, slapping my knee again for emphasis. "Step down, step down. What do they call you?"

My mind galloped. "Aruun," I mumbled in a deep voice. Stiffly I dismounted, fiery pains shooting through my legs as my numbed feet hit the frozen ground. My breath caught in my throat. I doubled over. Reaching to brace myself against Bayan, my hand fell against air, for she was already being led away. Wobbling, I paused to catch my breath. I could see Genma squinting again but, as before, her suspicious look was barely a ripple in her chatter.

"And I have the two most beautiful daughters! You must meet them! There is Otgon. She has seen eight summers and can milk my mares even faster than her sister— that is Davasuren. Now she has seen ten summers but already she is preparing the meals with me, and the man who takes her for his wife will grow as fat as I am. Hah!" Genma clasped her round belly. "Ten summers is still young, I think, for marriage, but in another year or two, perhaps . . . ?" She let her voice trail off.

"Delger," she called. "Unsaddle them both and turn them out. And give the mare a handful of that good grain. But watch, no more than a handful. It's too dear." Then, slapping me on the back, sending me stumbling toward the door, she said, "Come on, Aruun. I'll wager you have some stories for us. And some new stories to us will be as good grain to your mare. Let's begin with your message. I will make a guess," she said, closing her eyes briefly, "that you are carrying it within a sealed leather pouch tied around your waist underneath your *del*." She opened her eyes. "Am I right?"

I nodded.

"Do you know what it says?"

I shook my head.

"Do you know what's inside the two bags you carry?"

I shook my head again. While Genma began a long list of speculation, I found myself held fast, almost cringing, just inside the first square room I had ever entered. You see, when I looked up and saw the giant trunks of trees stretching close over my head I feared they would fall and crush me. But another powerful shove from Genma pushed me, stumbling again, right underneath them into the center of the room.

Looking around, wide-eyed, I saw that the walls, too, were stacks of tree trunks stuck together with dried mud. Sheets of wool felt, stirring slightly in the drafts, hung on each wall.

Two girls knelt beside the cooking fire, one stirring a broth bubbling within a footed bronze pot while the other pulled needle and thread through a *del* the color of dried grass. Heads bent together, smiles flashing wide in the firelight, they whispered gaily, bursting forth in the high, tinkling laughter of brass bells. Although I knew I was the source of their amusement, a part of me longed to throw off my heavy coverings and kneel, giggling, beside them. But I remained behind my mask.

In the far left corner of the room knelt a boy scraping an ox hide with energetic yet haphazard strokes. There was something odd about him. Already he was fat, like his mother, and from his profile he looked to be about my age. But he didn't even look up when I fell stumbling into the room.

While Genma busied herself pulling bowls from a tall blue cabinet, I continued gazing, open-mouthed, at my surroundings. Beds ringed the room, their iron feet sinking into thick *shirdiks* woven in colorful patterns of birds and flowers. At the foot of each bed rested a stocky wooden chest, festooned with designs of cranes and sheep, horses and leaves. The one nearest the two girls yawned open, revealing piles of richly dyed clothing. Near Genma, atop another large painted chest, slumped several dolls. I shuddered once, remembering the dirty-faced doll in my own *ger*. At the door hung a large goatskin bag, foaming with the familiar *ayrag,* and propped against the left wall were three of the most handsome saddles I had ever seen. Above them hung four or five fancy bridles and several tasseled breast collars and cruppers. I longed to trace my fingers across the beautiful craftsmanship, but at that moment Genma swayed around, silky *del* rustling, and clapped her hands.

"Aruun," she said, "we are ready. Since my husband is—my, my, my," she interrupted herself. "I have not introduced you to my daughters. Aruun, this is my first daughter, Davasuren, and this is her sister, Otgon." Each of the girls shyly nodded in turn. Genma did not introduce the boy in the corner.

She went on. "Aruun, since my husband is away—he is riding with the soldiers—you will have the seat of honor." She pointed to a fringed cushion behind the cooking fire, the seat facing the door and the one traditionally awarded to a guest.

Nodding, I took a step toward the cushion, but while my one leg was already tingling with newfound warmth, my crippled foot and ankle still throbbed painfully, so that I lurched forward like a still-wet ox calf. The sisters shared whispers again, but this time their laughter was cut short by the stern hushing of their mother. Just as I collapsed, red-faced, on the cushion, Delger came in and silently sat cross-legged on my right side. Steam rising from the cooking pot polished Genma's face as she began ladling the marmot stew into gleaming, bluish white bowls.

Now, I had never before seen porcelain. When a bowl was placed in my cupped hands, I yelped, and juggled and bobbled the fire-hot piece into my lap. Quick as a dog, I set to licking my burnt flesh. Genma glanced sidelong at me, her fat lips curled in a little smile, as she continued filling bowls for Delger and her two daughters. I watched each of them slip their hands back inside their sleeves, then expertly grasp the hot bowl with the padded comfort of their *dels*. Finally Genma ladled a bowlful for herself, then dragged a bright orange stool with four sturdy legs to the fire and lowered her weight to it.

When I noticed that all faces were turned toward me, expectant, I took a quick sip of the stew. Genma's boast of good cooking flew straight as an arrow. My heart quickened with the thought that her boast of fast horses might fly just as true.

Delger and the two girls lifted their bowls and began to suck noisily. That is, until a tsk-tsking noise from their mother, along with a raised eyebrow, made the older girl set her bowl aside, pick up yet another bowl—this one wooden—and ladle a half-portion into it. Wrinkling her nose, she rose and carried it to her brother in the corner.

I watched her place his chubby hands around the rim. She spoke a word to him, then returned to the fire and her own bowl.

The wind whistling through the cracks in the walls delivered a shrill whinny. I recognized it as Bayan's and a pang of worry for her safety and for Bator's—if he was even alive—stabbed my stomach. Looking from face to face, each one buried in the steam of a cupped bowl, I wondered about my own safety.

Although my place near the fire was hot, I kept my father's hat pulled low on my head, trying to ignore the sweat dampening my hair to my cheeks. It was then that I saw in the nervous glances of the others that these people were equally uncertain of me.

From beneath the creaking orange stool scurried a long-legged spider, headed across the *shirdik*. Genma stamped her trunk of a leg upon it. "Tell us about yourself, Aruun," she commanded. "Of what clan are you?"

I swallowed. "Kerait," I answered under my breath.

"Kerait?" she repeated. "Then you live west of here. You ride a long way from home. Are there many in your family?"

I shook my head.

"Do you have a wife?"

I shook my head again, sipping the broth and plopping black lumps of marmot meat into my mouth. I tried to look shy, which wasn't difficult. But Genma, like all people living far from their kind, had endless questions.

"Tell us, Aruun. How did you come to serve Kublai Khan?" She casually swirled the broth within her bowl, watching the liquid with one eye, me with the other. I busied myself with chewing a fatty chunk of meat, then raised the bowl to my lips for a long, thoughtful sip.

"We don't see too many of the Khan's arrow riders out this way," Genma went on, "but I have seen a few in my years." She squinted at me again, the way a cat ponders how close to sneak upon a mouse without sending it running. "Now, the ones I've seen dress differently from you," she was saying. "So I'm wondering why you're different." She smiled.

I lowered the empty bowl, wiped my mouth with my sleeve. I felt my face grow very hot. I was cornered.

"I . . . I was riding east of . . . of . . ." My words unexpectedly widened into a long yawn.

"Hah!" the woman laughed, slapping her knee. "The lid fits the pot, doesn't it? Go for moon after moon waiting for news and just when it walks in the door I worry it to a yawn with my questions. Please forgive me once again, Aruun. If you are finished"—a loud belch punctuated Genma's heaving her weight to her feet—"I'll take your bowl and you can take that bed in the corner." A flick of wrist and thumb indicated a small bed next to where the odd boy sat. "There's an extra blanket folded underneath if you get cold. I'll wake you at first light so you may be on your way."

Nodding appreciatively, and feigning another long yawn, I gave my bowl one last lick, then rose and limped toward the bed.

"May Tengri watch over your sleep," Genma called.

I fell upon the bed with a sigh that floated around the room. The dead could be no more tired, I thought, as I turned my back to the fire and pulled a heavy woven blanket across it. But my shoulders hunched instinctively at the loud whispering that erupted behind them and I began to worry again.

I was fairly certain that Genma suspected my identity

as an arrow rider, which posed two problems. If she discovered I was a girl, she would undoubtedly take the *paiza*
from me and keep me from riding south. Yet if she did
believe I was the Khan's messenger, she would make me
continue riding in the morning on a fresh horse, leaving
Bayan behind. Somehow I had to find a way to keep
both the *paiza* and Bayan and still deliver the Khan's
valuables—swiftly!

I sighed once more. How could I possibly ride Bayan
so soon? I knew I had pushed her too hard. What if her
leg was beyond healing? And what about Bator? What had
happened to him?

I heard Genma ask Delger to play the *morinkhour*, and
as he drew out the first hesitant notes, I began forming a
plan. Long before dawn, I decided, I would sneak out of
the station and place my saddle upon one of Genma's
horses. I would quickly look around for Bator, then lead
Bayan as fast as she could travel, hoping that without the
weight of a rider she would be able to make it. If she
couldn't, I hoped to leave her in the temporary care of
another clan. Then I would carry the Khan's bags of
treasure southward, to the next station and the next. In
my grand plans that night I even hoped that Kublai Khan
would be so pleased by my prompt delivery that he would
reward me with one of his own swift horses. Already I
could see myself returning to my *ail*, with both Bayan and
a beautiful, new horse to win the long race. Then I would
breed it and raise more swift horses, and every year after,
it would be one of my horses that won the long race.

Delger continued coaxing a melody from the strings,
the liquid notes fingering up my back and neck, then
plunging, warm, to the pit of my stomach. I rolled over
to watch him. He knelt, eyes closed, leaning almost affec-

tionately into the horse-headed instrument. Otgon and Davasuren nestled close to their mother, enveloped in her great arms.

And then I noticed the younger son. He was still seated in the corner, legs crossed, just at the foot of my bed. Large dark eyes, kind ones, like those of a cow, stared unblinking into the wall. He was rocking back and forth with the music. I noticed that his wooden bowl of marmot stew sat, still uneaten, in his lap. And then I saw why.

With both hands he would clutch the bowl's rim but, as he lifted it shakily to his lips, an unexpected twitch in one or both arms would nearly upend it. On his smooth chubby face I saw the raw emotions: the hunger to eat, the fear of dirtying himself, the pain of being different. Oh, how I recognized that pain. And I couldn't help myself.

Aware that all faces turned toward me, I slipped out of my bed and knelt beside the boy. I placed my hands over his. Looking into his eyes and nodding reassuringly, I helped him guide the bowl to his lips. He slurped hungrily. As we lowered the bowl together, he smiled. I smiled back and we lifted the bowl again.

Crouching in the corner's shadows then, knee to knee, we both listened, swaying, to the music. And each pull of the bow across the strings was a hard tug at my heart.

In the *morinkhour*'s haunting melodies I heard the trilling nicker of Bayan's greeting. Upon its music I was carried back to the windswept hill where I used to sit beside her all afternoon. I smelled the warm dust of her coat, the sage-scented breezes fingering her white mane, my long black hair. I remembered with that sweet yet bitter taste how it was to feel like the only two creatures in this world.

Delger began to hum a tune, his deep voice smooth and

soothing. I began to look upon him with new eyes. I admired the roundness of his head, black hair cropped short. My eyes noticed his furrowed brow, lingered upon his full lips pressed thoughtfully together. Then he began to sing. It was a song about a man who had two golden horses with manes of silver. One dark night this man's enemy crept up to the herd and stole the two horses. A long time passed and somehow one golden horse managed to return to its owner, but only this one horse. The man was very sad, but the horse was sadder.

The night's cold was pressing upon the room now and since the boy had long since finished his meal, I eased his head from my shoulder and crawled into bed. I listened to a few more songs, letting them fly me to mountaintops or gallop alongside princesses, and soon they carried me off to sleep.

17. Discovered!

*A*lready I was leaping the last creek, urging my horse on with shouts, for I heard the other riders pouring down the hillside behind me. The crowd parted, banners waving, hands clapping, feet pounding, pounding, pounding. . . .

The rhythmic thunder was growing louder and louder. Instinct jolted me awake. Sitting up, confused, I heard the stomping approach. A long grunt broke through my fog, the now-familiar scraping sounds of Genma's bulk squeezing through the doorway announcing her presence. Blinking the sleep from my eyes, I saw that she was leading the odd boy, stumbling, behind her. And slung over her meaty arm dangled one indignant tiger cat. I moved my mouth but no words came out.

"Well!" Genma said, a mysterious smile tugging at her lips. "At the very least you haven't died in my bed." Still clutching the chubby hand of her son, she gently released Bator, who scrambled headfirst down the great expanse of berry-colored silk. He padded across the *shirdik,* loudly meowing his complaints. "Now I'm wondering," Genma continued, "would this half-starved little creature that my daughters had to scoop from one of the milk bags belong to you?" Bator, by then, had leaped to my side, butting his head against my palm. I briskly rubbed the stiff hairs of his face, moist with droplets of milk. Looking at Genma, I nodded.

"Any other secrets you'd like to share?" The fat woman looked at me with one raised eyebrow while she removed the boy's soiled *del,* then guided his hands into a clean one pulled from one of the fancy chests.

Under her gaze I realized the cold morning air was sifting through my cropped hair and chilling my bare neck: my father's hat had fallen to the floor during the night. And there was a cold spot on my belly as well, an empty place where the leather pouch carrying the Khan's message was supposed to lie. My searching hands confirmed that both it and the gold *paiza* were missing. Widened eyes wordlessly told Genma I knew I had been discovered. I slowly nodded again, my heart pounding like that of an animal facing the hunter's arrow.

Genma led the boy waddling to a corner of the room and set him down, placing his hands around a bowl and large wooden spoon. Immediately he began to rock back and forth, banging out an uneven rhythm.

Then, hands upon her broad hips, Genma came and stood over me. She waited. And words came spilling from my mouth into the empty space between us.

"The pouch . . . with the Khan's message . . . and the *paiza* . . . they're gone!" I croaked. I was surprised to see that when Genma had drawn near to my bed, Bator had jumped down and begun affectionately polishing his coat against the large woman's *del.* She didn't kick him away.

"Now, those words," she said, not unkindly, "are the

truth. And maybe the first true words you've spoken to me. But you need not worry. I have them. And as soon as my son Delger returns from the temple, he'll carry the bags to the next station."

"But I am the Khan's arrow rider," I said, the tone of my voice rising with my growing fear. "He is expecting me to deliver them."

"He is expecting *you*—Aruun?" Genma drew out the false name suspiciously. "I don't know how you came to put a hand on the royal *paiza* of Kublai Khan, but I'm as certain as salt he is not expecting you. Which makes me think there's more to your story than what you've told us—Aruun."

My own lie echoing in my ears, I sighed. "Oyuna," I corrected, actually relieved to shed my poor-fitting disguise. Red-faced, I picked up my father's hat and shyly turned my eyes toward Genma. "Was it the hat?"

"Hah!" she snorted, the golden rings of fat jiggling at her neck. "A woman doesn't bear four children from her loins and not know the difference between the girls and the boys—hat or no hat. Although," she added shyly, "unfastening your *del* to get at the message pouch did reveal more than your nakedness." Annoyance suddenly clouded Genma's face. "I only took those things because you were dead to the world with sleep and I wanted Delger to ride on with the Khan's bags. They won't be delayed at my station." She snorted again. "But he said it's an important day at the temple and rode there instead."

"I'll ride on with the bags," I began, but Genma cut me off.

"You're only a girl and you'll do no such thing," she said sharply. She turned to pull bowls from the tall blue cabinet and as quickly as she turned back the irritation in her voice vanished. "Now, then, since I did not get my story last night, I believe I deserve twice the story this morning. And somehow I'm willing to wager I'm going to get it." She tossed me a sunny smile. "Come, now," she said. "I have some tea and millet boiled for your breakfast—well, closer to calling it lunch but we won't send an arrow rider with that news. What do you take in it? Butter? Milk?"

"Both, please," I answered, pushing the covers away. A chill air encircled my legs. I wondered why I hadn't felt its cold last night when the covers had been pulled from me by a stranger. I shivered, for I had never felt so vulnerable, even when I was riding with the soldiers. One hand felt for and found the comforting weight of my lucky gold ornament, still hidden within my *del*. The fingers of my other hand tentatively tunneled through my short hair, which hung, dirty and unbraided, around my ears. It felt strange, for no woman of my tribe had ever cut her hair short. For a moment, a panicky feeling of not knowing just who I was swept across me.

"Is that the new fashion of the Kerait?" Genma teased.

I squirmed, pulling on my boots. "I must see to my horse," I said.

Genma ignored me, carrying two porcelain bowls to the fire and lifting the pot from the coals. "To *your* horse?" she said. "Or the Khan's horse? Whichever you decide to tell me, the white mare you rode in on is fine. I've seen to her already this morning. She's a bit puffed up on her far hind leg, so my girls are wrapping it in a blue gentian poultice. But you won't be riding her for a few days."

"I have to," I blurted in alarm.

Genma shot me a look while continuing to ladle millet into the bowls. "You won't," she said firmly. "The old mare needs a rest. Delger can ride out at first light." She dropped a chunk of butter into each bowl, then drizzled creamy milk over both. "Come," she said, waving a hand.

I left my bed to slump beside the cooking fire. Bator followed, flopping across my lap and purring happily. Slipping my hands inside my sleeves, I accepted the delicate bowl. Pale blue horses galloped endlessly around it.

"I must deliver the Khan's treasure," I said, eyeing the twin goatskin bags near the doorway. "And swiftly. And I have to take Bayan with me."

Genma pulled the sturdy orange stool to the fire and, grunting, squatted on it. "Who?" she asked after a sip from her own tea bowl.

"Bayan, my white mare. I have to take her with me. And she is mine," I said, glaring at my doubter over an outthrust jaw. "My father paid silver coins for her at Karakorum."

"All right, all right. I believe you." Genma began to chuckle. "You and your cat there, you both have your stubborn ways. I suppose he has a name as well?" She tipped her head toward the striped cat sprawled belly-up in my lap.

My own lips twitched. "Of course," I responded. "His name is Bator."

"Bator? You mean 'Hero'? That little thing? Hah!" Genma slapped her knee and bounced forward and back. "That's the start of a good story and worthy of more tea. Please help yourself.'

I poured some more tea atop the remaining millet swirling in the bottom of my bowl.

"My, my, my," Genma said. "So you gave your cat the name Bator and you gave your horse a name as well. I never heard of such a thing. What was the mare's name again?"

"Bayan."

"Yes, Bayan. And why did you give her a name?"

"Because my cat already had a name and I didn't want to hurt my mare's feelings."

I had tried to say those words with a straight face, but already the laughter was bubbling up within me and both Genma and I doubled over in guffaws.

"Hah!" Genma laughed. "Hah! Well, that's as good a reason as any, I guess, to give a name to something that isn't a person. I don't understand it, but I certainly do accept it. But tell me, Oyuna, what is a young girl like yourself doing so far from home with a sore-legged horse and a . . . a hungry cat!" She was set to laughing again, for Bator had suddenly appeared at her side, licking traces of butter from her fingers.

"I told you," I said, my face truly serious. "I am delivering the Khan's treasure."

"Ah, yes. But does the Khan know you are delivering it? In my experience arrow riders, like my son Delger, are all boys. Just how did you come to risk your neck in the name of Kublai Khan? And why do you think I would let this bird-witted venture of yours continue?"

I had no choice then but to tell Genma how I had disguised myself as my stepbrother to stay with Bayan and why I had been given the Khan's twin bags. Genma listened to my story with respect and I ended up telling her more about the way Bayan spoke to me than I had intended. When I finished, Genma nodded approvingly.

"Well told, Oyuna. I admire your loyalty. And you have earned your dinner." She smiled. "Marmot again. I hope you liked it."

I nodded enthusiastically, for my mouth already watered at the thought.

"Now, you may be surprised to hear this," Genma went

on, "but I do believe your mare spoke to you. I won't run to the mountaintop and shout it to the wind—." She snorted. "Well, that's a waste of words, for I can't run anyway," she said, chuckling a little. "But what I mean to say is, I'm sure most people wouldn't believe you. And I don't advise telling just everyone you meet that you carry on conversations with your horse." She looked at me sternly and I nodded.

"But I do understand," she said. Bracing her hands on her legs, Genma leaned back. "Over the years I have owned some favorite horses. None that I've given a name to"—she cocked her head at me and grinned—"but I felt we were of one spirit. When I watched them gallop, my heart galloped with them. Oh, how I longed to sit upon one's back and watch the ground fly past me but"—looking down, she snorted again—"it would take three or more horses harnessed together to carry this body." The woman sighed, yet a small fire burned in her eyes. "So I worked with them from the ground. I studied their blood, and I chose which mare to breed to which stallion. Very careful was I, not just turning loose my mares, as I have heard they do in the north. I was careful. And I watched to see which stallion could stamp his likeness on his foals and which mare could pass on her steady disposition. I watched, especially, for strong legs—a short cannon and a long forearm—and, of course, small hard hooves. For these qualities make for very fast horses." Genma sucked in her breath and smiled. "But listen to me prattle on." She laughed. "Might as well try to tell the stream to stop running once you get me talking about my horses."

I smiled over my tea bowl, for I understood.

"Tell me one thing, Oyuna," Genma said, looking directly at me. "You left your family in order to stay with Bayan. Now you have her. Why do you not ride for home?"

I hadn't told Genma about my bad luck. Maybe if I didn't speak about it, I thought, or think about it, it wouldn't find me here. So I said simply, "I'm looking for a swift horse, one to win a race. Someone told me there is a herd of ten thousand white mares south of here. Is it true?"

Genma nodded. "Yes, I have heard that Kublai Khan keeps ten thousand white mares."

My ears pricked. I was doubly determined to deliver his treasure.

"And he keeps an equal number of white cows," Genma went on. "He believes the mares carry luck and uses their milk in ceremonies. No one may disturb his herds—even if they are blocking a road, you must ride around them, even if that ride costs another half-day; no one may bother these white animals." Now Genma turned her head toward the two goatskin bags. She frowned. "The Khan always gets what he wants and he should be getting these right now." She stamped her leg. "That Delger! Chasing his dreams is going to get us all killed."

18. Genma's Dreams

Genma abruptly ended our conversation. A long silence crept by while she stared at the *shirdik*. Then, keeping her thoughts to herself, she fashioned a sunny smile and asked if I wanted to see Bayan now. Of course I nodded happily and Bator and I followed her out and around the station house to a sheltered meadow. Several horses, hobbled for ready saddling, grazed contentedly amid a small flock of black-and-white-spotted sheep.

Bayan, however, stood apart. Even with both front legs hobbled and a hind leg wrapped in a poultice-stained bandage, she shuffled anxiously from side to side. She was peering intently toward the thicket to the south and I thought at first she was looking for Bator; but when he ran up, she gave him only a quick sniff before returning to her nervous weaving.

"What's gotten under her hide?" Genma asked.

I shrugged. "I don't know." But I could feel Bayan's uneasiness stirring the hairs on the back of my neck. Something was wrong.

Genma turned her attention to the whereabouts of her two daughters and left my side calling their names. Neither Bayan nor Bator flicked an ear to her voice as the little cat joined the mare in staring into the distance. With a concerned frown I moved toward Bayan, hand outstretched. The moment my fingers touched her shoulder she whinnied loudly. I jumped. Bator looked up, meowed, and looked away.

"What's wrong?" I murmured, scratching the fuzzy white neck in big, soothing circles. Bayan shook all over, continued shuffling. I looked down at Bator. "What is it?" He ignored me, although his mouth opened and he began to pant rapidly. Following the eyes of my two friends, I squinted toward the thicket. Nothing was coming that I could see.

Or was it that the two wanted to be going? The path leading to the next arrow station stretched into this thicket. My heart bounded as I remembered Genma confirming what Echenkorlo had told me: ten thousand white mares waited to the south. I was certain I would find my swift horse among them. Observing Bayan's leg, I noticed some stiffness, but no serious lameness, although shuffling was hardly galloping. And if my plan was to work, we would have to gallop—fast and hard.

I retreated to the shade of a large pine tree to study Bayan's leg further and to go over the details of my plan. Genma ignored me as she waddled back to the station house followed by Otgon and Davasuren. The girls appeared some time later carrying milking bags and disappeared over a small rise. They returned—and this I found strange—to unhobble the horses and lead them over the rise. Pounding hooves signaled their release. Only Bayan and the sheep were left in the meadow.

Not until late afternoon did Genma call my name. Bayan

had finally ceased her shuffling, though she lifted her head between snatches of grass to continue staring southward. Bator had moved to my lap, but he, too, was keeping a watchful eye on the path through the thicket. He didn't even complain when I dumped him to the ground to answer Genma's summons.

The moment I entered the station house I could tell that Genma's fitful nature had shifted to the stormy side. Everyone was working in silence—Davasuren lugging in fresh water and Otgon beating the *ayrag*—while Genma rocked upon her orange stool, muttering to herself as she stirred the cooking pot. I saw the girls exchange knowing glances. The odd son sat in his corner as usual, but even he remained quiet. That prickly feeling crept up my back. When at last we sat down to eat, all eyes darted apprehensively back and forth to Genma's scowling face. Not until halfway through the meal did she speak. And then it was bluntly.

"Is it your crippled foot that has kept you from marrying?"

Heat rushed to my face. Slowly I nodded.

"Did your father—I assume you still have one—ever try to arrange a marriage?"

I nodded again. "At last year's festival at Karakorum," I whispered. "But no one would have me."

Genma stared into her bowl, rhythmically swirling the broth for several long breaths. Then she raised her head, pulled herself as tall as her wide frame would allow, and, in a voice full of authority, said, "You will marry my son Delger."

The daughters and I gasped in unison. "But he wants—" began Davasuren.

"Hush!" ordered Genma. She emptied her uneaten

stew into the cooking pot, dangerously rapping the porcelain bowl on the bronze rim. Setting it aside, she dragged
the kettle of boiling water from the embers and plopped
a chunk of tea leaves into it. "I know Delger wants to be
a lama," Genma said evenly, though she glared at her
elder daughter, "but I want babies in my house. Now! It
will be two or three more years before you marry and
leave me to go live with your husband, even longer for
Otgon." The hungry dark eyes swept over the head of
her younger daughter, coming to rest upon my equally
stunned face. "But it is past time for Delger. How many
springs have you seen, Oyuna?"

"Nearly thirteen," I croaked.

"Past time for you as well. The gods have smiled upon
me by guiding you to my house—and they well know how
few women have passed through this door flap. You have
been sent by them to be my daughter-in-law." Genma
leaned forward, quivering with excitement. "You find my
son handsome, don't you?"

Again I flushed, for I remembered how, just last night,
I had admired Delger's round head, his thick lips, his
sensitive fingers. To marry such as him would be any
girl's dream. But marriage, I now knew, was not his dream.

"Well, don't you?" Genma prodded.

I looked up. Truthfully I said, "It would be an honor
to be Delger's wife. But if it is his dream to be a lama,
then—"

"Dreams!" Genma spat the word. "Dreams aren't for
the likes of us." She pulled one of the coral carvings
from her ear, tugged on the fleshy lobe, then replaced the
earring. "Delger dreams of becoming a lama—and him
with those thick, dirty fingers! Well, even I know you
have to own beautiful hands to be a lama, for singing the

songs. And you!" Just like a spring storm, the woman's temper unexpectedly blew in my direction. "You tell me you're dreaming of riding right up to the Khan's palace and handing him his treasure. Well," she said, leaning forward and lowering her voice as if she shared a secret, "my eyes may be growing cloudy, but they can still see that you're a cripple, Oyuna, and last I knew they don't welcome the ugly and infirm into the presence of Kublai Khan."

Satisfied with her outburst, Genma sat back upon her creaking stool and began to pour tea. For her, the skies had cleared. "The sooner you give up hoping for something that's not going to happen, the happier you'll be," she said matter-of-factly. She handed me a tea bowl, with a warm smile. "Now, you just plan to stay here with my family and you and Delger can have lots of babies and you'll both see just how nice life is to live."

Genma abruptly changed the subject then, turning to Davasuren to ask about the number of lambs expected this spring. My hands trembled as I cupped my tea bowl and turned over Genma's words. She was partly right, I admitted. I, a girl—and yes, a cripple—had no business riding to the royal city of Khanbaliq. I didn't even know how far it was, or exactly where.

The image of Delger's handsome face flashed in my mind. Where else would I find such a husband? Ever so slightly I shook my head. Delger was at the temple at that very moment, against his mother's wishes, because he wanted to learn to be a lama. It wasn't his dream to marry and—I was growing more confident now—it wasn't mine either. My heart's true desire lay to the south. I had to ride on.

I probably would not have spoken another word that

evening, having so much to think about, but Bayan's strange behavior continued. Somehow she managed to nose her way inside the slanting storage shed next to the station. Ripping open a bag of grain, she scattered the precious foodstuff all over the ground, gorging for no one knows how long. It wasn't until well after dinner, when we were just heading for our beds, that a suspicious noise made Genma send Davasuren to investigate. When the girl returned to report the spillage, Genma's face again grew stormy. My frantic apologies fell on deaf ears as the woman rose, pulled a short knife from the cabinet, and stomped into the darkness.

I think Genma enjoyed "treating" Bayan that night. Saying that the horse's blood would be too rich carrying all that grain, the huge woman twisted my mare's upper lip with one strong fist and, by the light of torches held by her daughters, poked the knife inside Bayan's mouth. After searching for just the right spot, Genma jabbed the glistening pink gum. I gulped, my stomach churning, as I watched the blood drip and drip from Bayan's gaping mouth. Genma showed no pity, even though the old mare groaned and writhed beneath her grip.

"Trust me," she muttered. "I know what is best."

The station was silent after that and we crawled beneath our covers with few words. Yet long after Genma and her family fell to snoring, I lay with my fingers rubbing at my collarbone, for I felt as if the herdsman's *urga* had tightened around my neck. I had to gallop from this place and it had to be tomorrow.

19. Bayan Is Lost to Me

I awakened in the still-dark, my escape plans instantly withering: Genma was gone from her bed. Hurriedly I pulled on my boots but before I could slip outside I heard the heavy footsteps approaching. The girls stirred, though neither they nor their younger brother arose. By the pinkish light sifting past Genma through the door flap, I saw that the sleeves of her berry-colored *del* were pushed to her elbows and that her meaty arms were smeared with blood.

She flinched, momentarily surprised at seeing me sitting upon the edge of my bed.

"May the sun shine upon you," she said in greeting. "Won't you stir up the cooking fire, dear one? I'll ready us some tea."

Reluctantly I poked at the embers with two dung cakes and, after adding my breath, coaxed a small fire. Genma and I were soon seated beside the flames, sipping tea, and while I tried to keep up with her chatter about horses I kept eyeing her bloody arms and wishing I was far, far away. One by one her children awakened and, yawning, took bowls in their hands to join us. I didn't realize I was still rubbing at my collarbone until Genma asked what was the matter. I could only throw up my hands and laugh weakly.

After breakfast Genma found one thing and then another to keep me at her side. She dug through a chest to show me an ancient and brittle silk scarf that had been carried all the way from Shangtu. Placing each of her delicate tea bowls one by one into my cupped hands, she told me when she had received each and the name of the rider who had given it to her. Genma went so far as to drape a length of pale, thistle-colored silk across my shoulder and promise to begin sewing me a new *del* the next day—as if I had already agreed to join her family!

In this manner the morning crawled along. Bator padded in and out, dozing in the moving circle of sunlight before, time and again, jumping up suddenly to skitter outside. I longed to follow him, but each time my eyes wandered, Genma slapped me upon the back and pulled another treasure and another story from her trunk.

When I could tell, even within the shadows of the arrow station, that the sun had risen high in the sky, I politely interrupted her ramblings. "Please," I said, "I must see to Bayan now. Pehaps her leg is better."

The large woman's face fell. Her shoulders rose and sank, expelling a long sigh. Squatting spraddle-legged on her orange stool, Genma motioned to me. "Come, Oyuna," she said somberly. "I have something to tell you."

Panic-stricken, I somehow managed to push my feet forward until I was engulfed in the meaty arms, pressed into the squashy bosom. Genma smothered me in her embrace while she rocked back and forth upon the squeaking stool.

"I'm sorry, Oyuna. Very, very sorry." She murmured these words into my ear. "But Bayan did not live the night. I found her near death this morning." Holding my trembling body at arm's length then, Genma looked into my face and said, "Too much grain. It was the kindest thing—ending her life. I know you would not have wanted her to feel any more pain."

I shook my head, a sick fear squeezing my heart. "No! I must see her. Where is she?"

"She is dead, Oyuna. There is nothing you can do. Better you stay inside here today until I can harness the ox and drag the body away."

"No!" I said again, shaking my head vigorously. "No! I won't. I must see her. You can't keep me here."

I twisted free of her grip. But with unexpected swiftness, Genma lunged toward the door frame and blocked my escape with her large body. "Oyuna," she said in a strangely calm voice, "I have known horses for many years more than you. I know what is best. Now, it's all right to cry, child. Why, I shed some tears myself when I found your poor old mare suffering so."

She sounded so caring, yet every bone in my body was telling me to run from that place.

"I understand how you feel, Oyuna," she was saying. "So you just go back and sit by the fire and we'll talk about your mare—about Bayan. You can tell me all about your days with her and after a long cry you'll feel better. And tomorrow will be better and the day after that and so on. You'll see."

At that moment, Bator rushed in between Genma's fat

ankles, looked around wildly, and bolted back outside. I had to follow him, I felt, or stay caught forever in Genma's greedy trap. My own quick glance around the room showed that my saddle and bridle were missing. So was the leather pouch given to me by Echenkorlo. And the Khan's twin goatskin bags.

But I still had the knife I had slipped into my boot on the day I had cut off my braid. Holding Genma's angry gaze, I slowly reached my hand inside my boot, found the small knife's iron handle, and pulled it out, aiming the point at the woman's fat middle. Genma's eyes widened.

"Oyuna!" she scolded in a mother's voice. "You put that down this instant. I won't have such behavior in my home."

"Let me out of here," I said between gritted teeth.

"Now, Oyuna," she began to say, but in one swipe her huge arm knocked my fist aside, sending the knife flying into the fire. With eerie precision it angled off the bronze cauldron, pierced the embers, and — most unlucky — stuck, small flames lapping at the handle. Genma gasped. The hairs on my neck stood stiff. Yet so determined was I to escape that place that I moved toward the knife anyway.

The rush of air at my side told me Genma's grasp had fallen short. "No!" she cried, still clinging to the door frame. "The knife has cut the fire. We must call the shaman!"

But I would not listen to her anymore. With the toe of my boot, I kicked the knife clear of the flames. Then I knelt, slipped my hand inside the sleeve of my *del,* and seized the hot handle. Heart pounding in my ears, I rose.

"Let me out now!" I said, again pointing the knife at Genma and taking a confident step toward her.

Fear blanched Genma's fat face, for now I threatened

her with bad luck as well as a weapon. Her small eyes hard on the blade, she eased her weight aside, giving up just enough daylight for me to dart past.

Outside I stumbled over the bloody carcass of a sheep, but gave it no mind when I saw that one of Genma's horses, a dapple gray gelding with two white stockings and a white belly patch, stood saddled and waiting. The bulging goatskin bags were slung across his back. At that instant I heard a leisurely clip-clopping and looked down the path to see Delger riding toward us. Genma was behind me now, waving and shouting for him to hurry. But he couldn't hear her. Cupping a hand to his ear, Delger rode up to the arrow station and reined to a surprised halt.

Brandishing my knife, I ordered the wide-eyed Delger to step from his horse and hobble it. While he was doing so, I spun around, slashing the knife wildly through the air. I could see the two sisters, open-mouthed, peeking at me from around the corner post. So fierce I must have appeared! Like an animal I crouched, lifting my lip to reveal clenched teeth.

A grunting noise made me spin, slash the air again. But it wasn't Genma. There at my feet, playing in the dirt, was the odd son. He was grinning at me and grunting, earnestly trying to tell me something. From behind his back then he pulled the leather pouch given to me by my grandmother and held it high in the air. For just a moment my fury melted. I smiled at him, squeezing his chubby hand as I took the pouch. I brandished the knife one last time at the others, then untied the gray's reins and stepped into the saddle. Thumping my heels, I galloped down the path and into the thicket.

"You don't know the way!" I heard Genma shout. "You won't make it through the mountains!"

You may be right, I silently answered. But at least I'm choosing my own path.

Fear and excitement washed through my veins as I bent over the neck of the sprinting horse. Jumbled pictures, pieces of thoughts blew through my mind like the wind through the whipping mane. Was I headed in the right direction? Would I be safe? What, in the name of Tengri, had happened to Bayan? And where was Bator?

Bounding uphill, galloping in grunting leaps, we shadowed the tumbling stream. Kept pushing, springing, until we climbed up and over the first rise, then pushed on again until we cleared the second rise. Only then did I pull the gray to a stop. He was blowing hard. Too hard. And a new fear began to strangle my stomach. This horse I sat upon, the one I needed to escape, was not fast. Genma's boasts fell short of their target. The poor animal's legs were trembling with the sudden effort. They carried neither strength nor stamina. Why, any one of my father's horses could outrace him.

Hidden from view in a brushy hollow lying between one rise and the next, I pulled Genma's horse into a circle, letting him find his breath while I held mine, listening for followers.

My ears heard no hoofbeats, no triumphant shouts of chase. But they did catch the far-off cry, carried on the breeze, of a small animal. I smiled at Bator's complaining. Although I itched to gallop farther away from Genma's arrow station, I waited.

Finally the tiger-striped cat bounded through the brush, pink tongue fluttering between loud meows. At least I had one of my friends back, though Genma's telling of Bayan's death chilled my heart.

"Come up, Bator," I said, patting my leg for him to jump into the saddle.

But the wailing animal ignored me. Blinking his upturned green eyes against the bright sunshine, Bator also circled anxiously, meowing, then turned away from the babbling stream to trot along the hollow. Biting my lip, fearful that we would still be caught, I reined in the gray behind the scurrying, stiff-tailed animal.

Not a dozen breaths later, a familiar whinny wafted through the air. Bayan! I was sure of it! I stood in my stirrups, looking, but I could not see her, for the mountainside slanting around me folded into gullies and rose into hillocks. Newly leafing bushes stretched their green branches across my face as if to further hinder my search. Bator was quickly trotting ahead, so I urged the gray to hurry up and follow him around the jagged base of a long, rocky slope. Before the horse responded, Bator disappeared.

I kicked my tired mount into a reluctant trot, turning my head this way and that. Suddenly the saddle dropped from under me. The gray, snorting and scrambling in alarm, was sliding on his haunches into a mud-slickened gorge. I could only sit deep and hope we safely reached bottom.

But the scare was worth it. For as I gathered the reins, patting the frightened horse on the neck, my eye caught something white moving within some large bushes. There, even though hobbled and tied to a branch, pranced my lovely white mare, Bayan. So beautiful was she just then— eyes black and alive, neck arching with pride, mane falling upon her shoulders like a silken robe. I practically tumbled out of the saddle in my eagerness to reach her; I ran my hands down her fine legs, slender as a gazelle's, to unfasten the coarse hobbles, then quickly untied her head and threw my arms around her fuzzy neck. Bayan nickered and rubbed her face against my shoulder.

Bator, too, was rubbing against me, still meowing, and I knew we had to hurry.

Leading the still-panting gray beside Bayan, I tied him to the branch in her place and slipped the hobbles upon his legs. Then I lifted the saddle from his back and fastened it upon Bayan's. I draped the Khan's heavy bags across it. After fitting the bridle into Bayan's mouth, I was ready.

This time when I called Bator into the saddle, he scrambled up my leg and balanced, crouched, in my lap. Giving Bayan her head, I let her pick an easy way up and out of the gorge. She moved willingly, with no hint of lameness, and shortly we were back climbing beside the tumbling stream.

So Genma had lied to me, I thought. She had hoped that if she took Bayan from me I would give up my dreams and stay and marry her son. But I won't give up my dreams, I said to myself. And, silently, I prayed that Delger would not give up his.

20. Our Heads Brush the Skies

*W*e threw ourselves at the mountains—Bayan, Bator, and I. Climbed enthusiastically toward the heavens: mystic realm of the shamans, home to the gods, opening to the otherworld. And to my mother. That thought rippled my spine with a shiver.

Bayan's furry white shoulders tirelessly bunched and released beneath me, grabbing at the steep slope and pushing it behind us. Head low, breath rhythmic, she poured her energy into gaining the top before nightfall. I was awed by her smooth power.

Bator, on the other hand, was all playfulness: springing recklessly through the undergrowth, pouncing upon bugs, crouching and wriggling before dashing madly ahead, then sitting and meowing, waiting for Bayan and me to catch up.

We had resumed our journey south. Its adventure filled the two animals with excitement. But I—I was full of dread. Trailing my fingers across my hip, I laid a hand upon the empty place where the Khan's gold *paiza*, my guarantee of safe passage, was missing. In my haste to escape with the goatskin bags, I had forgotten to take both the message pouch and the gold *paiza*. Now I was just another person riding through the land; no longer did I carry the protection of the Khan as his arrow rider.

Nor did I carry with me any food, or any sure directions—other than a hint to follow the stream—to lead me to the city of Khanbaliq. How was I ever going to find Kublai Khan and my swift horse?

And there was something else, something that made me flinch with each thorny bush that snatched at my trousers, made me jump with each twig that snapped beneath Bayan's hooves. The bad luck. My bad luck. I was sure I could feel its icy breath skimming the back of my neck.

When my knife had cut through Genma's fire, it and the arrow station had become unclean. She had been right. We should have stopped and sent for the shaman. But no. I had boldly kicked the tainted knife from the fire and, holding it close to me, raised it as a weapon.

I had been trying to ignore it all afternoon, certain we could outclimb it, but now, glancing over my shoulder for the hundredth time, I saw my bad luck chasing after us in the form of angry gray storm clouds. At that moment, a flash of lightning lit the rapidly darkening sky. Thunder rumbled up the mountainside, nipping at our heels. I shrank in the saddle. Maybe an offering to the mountain spirit would save us. Reaching trembling fingers inside my boot, I lifted the small iron knife away from me and let it drop. The slope's webby undergrowth swallowed the tainted weapon and Bayan's powerful pace quickly carried us past it. But that wasn't enough.

A blue-white bolt of lightning crashed directly overhead, firing the sky. In its blinding glare I saw the stiff, waxy face of my mother lying in the mud. Fear gnawed my bones. My mother had died because of her daughter's bad luck. Was I leading Bayan and Bator into the same fate?

Again I heard thunder roar louder and louder until its deafening boom shook the mountain. At our backs this time hissed another bolt of lightning; I cringed. Squeezing shut my eyes, I hunkered over Bayan's neck.

And then the heavens split open, drenching us in a pounding rain. Bator gave up his games to crawl, sodden and shivering, into my lap. Though she had to pick her way more carefully now, Bayan kept climbing. The mucky sound of hooves sloshing through mud changed to the clacking sound of hooves striking upon stone. We were working our way higher. An occasional misstep upon the slick rock caused Bayan's hip to slump, nearly unseating both Bator and me, but still the determined white mare climbed on.

The rain grew heavier and colder with nightfall. The hard drops pelleted my bare head, stung the burning tops of my ears. They turned to ice in my hair and began forming thick snakes of ice in Bayan's mane. I had long ago lost any feeling in my toes. And though, blinking the water from my eyes, I could see the reins entwined around my fingers, I could not feel their leather. I was as wet as if I had plunged into a river, fully clothed. Shivering without control, my knees banged weakly against the sides of the saddle.

Rain and night slowly engulfed the mountain. Finally I could not see an arm's length in front of me. The path ahead, if there was one, swam in darkness. For all I knew we were climbing straight into the murky otherworld of the dead.

I felt Bayan twist sharply beneath me and suddenly a rocky wall was scraping my knee, ripping at my trousers. Sucking in my breath, I tried to flatten my leg, but the pressure kept building. Even Bayan was acting nervous now. She stopped and started in fitful leaps, hooves scrambling on loose pebbles. Then she would pause, swinging her nose this way and that against the black veil of rain, snorting, before frantically jumping again into the void. A useless passenger, I could only clutch the clawing, ear-flattened Bator to my lap and trust the instincts of my white mare. Tree branches no longer brushed my cheeks and shoulders. And even before the mind-numbing rain, I had lost the stream's reassuring babble. A dizziness in my head joined a sickness in my stomach to warn that we balanced high upon the mountain slope. But with the blackness all around us I could see nothing. Nothing!

Bayan lunged forward again. But this time her hooves scrambled helplessly as her weight lurched sideways. I suddenly felt myself being pulled down as she stumbled to her knees, plunged onto her shoulder. My leg was pinned beneath the mare and the rocky slope as we began sliding—fast—the mountain ripping through my skin as easily as it ripped through my *del,* searching for bone. Amid the drumming blows to my head, my elbow, my hip, I somehow knew Bator leaped free. But I was pinned beneath a crushing weight—and falling, falling, falling into darkness.

How long it was before I knew the mountain had stopped sliding beneath my fingernails, I don't know. The rain had ceased, and when I became aware of the cold mud painting my cheek, the grit lodged under my tongue, I tried to rise. Stabbing pains, like ice into flesh, pierced my ribs and ankle. I exhaled in brief, gasping breaths, clawing the wet earth and wondering at the bits of light twirling overhead. Gradually the white dots slowed, floating, then stuck hard in the raven's wing pressed so close to my face. I remember putting up my hand, wanting to touch the silky blackness. Instead, a whiteness pushed away the night, a warm softness blew upon my upstretched fingers.

Bayan! She was standing over me, nudging my hand with her soft muzzle. I felt my fingers trace the puckering lips, find the curving jawbone, climb to the cheekbone, stumble into the lashes and the liquid eye. Startled, Bayan jerked away. My hand dropped to the ground, limp, and I let the black wing fall across me once more.

How long I lay, eyes unseeing a second time, I still don't know. Gradually I became aware of a buzzing in my ear, like that of a winged bug, prodding me awake. Yet before I opened my eyes, the buzzing turned to sounds, the sounds to words.

"It is not done."

I blinked my eyes open. Again the stars slowed and stuck. Bayan stretched her neck down and blew warm gusts across my face.

"It is not done."

I heard the words again. Or thought I heard them. Frowning, I looked into Bayan's dark eyes. Then other words flooded my mind. I heard Echenkorlo talking: "Every living thing has a voice. . . . This white mare has spoken to you because she knew you would hear her. And you must listen."

Bayan nuzzled me again, gently butting my shoulder with her muzzle. And then Bator was there as well, licking my nose with his scratchy tongue, walking across my chest and meowing.

I didn't want to get up. I wanted to give up. Yet by

some will stronger than my own I rolled onto my side, nearly screaming in pain and, panting shakily, managed to rise onto one knee.

My eyes remained tightly shut, for the wounds were gnashing their teeth into me with frightening fury. Still, I could hear Bayan's hooves step closer. The leather stirrup bumped my head. Gritting my teeth, I strung an arm through it and pulled myself off the ground. Then, trying not to think about blood and broken bones and spiritless bodies shriveled upon the ground, I continued pulling myself up and into the saddle, finally collapsing with a groan over its arching front. Carrying little more than a crumpled carcass then, Bayan moved off into the darkness. I thought I heard Bator's faint mew, though it sounded very far away.

And then we were climbing again. Each rhythmic lunge upward stabbed fresh torture into my broken body. Bayan moved with confidence now, no more blind leaps into a dark downpour. A newborn moon peeked through silver-edged clouds, shedding a wet light upon rock washed clean of twigs and leaves.

At last we were up. So long had we been climbing that Bayan's first steps upon flat ground felt as if we floated upon air. With a fog drifting at our feet, I thought with a shiver that perhaps we had climbed right through the clouds into the heavens.

Bayan halted. A thick silence hung over the dampened mountaintop. In its eerie emptiness Bayan stamped a hoof and snorted. Then she shook all over, almost unseating me. Ears pricked into the darkness, she whinnied loudly. I cocked an ear as well, but the mare's call, shrouded by the fog, went unanswered.

A fresh spattering of rain blew across my face. I had to

find shelter, I thought. Chilled, aching all over, and soaked to the skin, I wouldn't survive another storm. But when my heels nudged Bayan, she refused to move. Was she injured, too? Or scared? Or just plain exhausted?

Out of the dark, Bator joined us again, his green eyes glinting in the moonlight. Bayan lowered her neck and touched her muzzle to his nose. They exchanged breaths. Then, lifting her head, the tired white mare took a confident step forward, following Bator through a sparse stand of pine trees. I remained the helpless passenger, doubled over her outstretched neck, clutching the saddle with icy hands.

I must have fallen asleep, for an unexpected crash of lightning jolted me awake. My heart boomed in my chest, more than matching the next rolling clap of thunder. No! Not again, I thought. I looked wildly around me. Another lightning bolt slashed through the sky, briefly throwing the mountaintop into stark silhouette. In that instant I caught sight of an oxcart, empty shafts resting upon the ground. Behind it—a small cave. I threw aside any apprehensions of the strangers crouching inside; at least I wouldn't spend the night alone!

Drumming Bayan's sides with my heels, I prodded her close to the cave entrance.

"Hello?" I called. "Hello?" There was no answer from within. Perhaps they were asleep, I thought. I called again, louder, and waited. Still no answer. Perhaps they had gone hunting. Should I, uninvited, enter the shelter of a stranger? Another bolt of lightning, hissing above my head, made the decision clear. I leaped from the saddle and scrambled just inside the cave's mouth.

The cavern yawned widely enough to shelter Bayan as well, so when the echoing thunder died down, I darted out to tug at the reins. Strangely, the white mare braced her full weight against them, refusing to take another step. So I forced my fingers, clumsy with cold, to pull the goatskin bags to the wet ground and unfasten the saddle and bridle. Bayan immediately ambled away, head to the ground, searching for grasses.

In two pain-filled trips I dragged the saddle, rug, bridle, and the Khan's twin bags inside the cave, still calling out in case someone slept within. No voice answered. Bator already huddled silently in the dirt, thin moonlight reflecting off the raindrops beading his coat.

Suddenly the tiring day and long, frightening night beat me to the ground. Bracing my bruised body against the cold rock wall, I shifted uncomfortably from one hip to the other, trying to ease the pain. The saddle rug was wet, but its thickness held Bayan's warmth and I pulled it over my legs. Bator climbed up my chest, licking my nose before curling upon my lap. In the next breath his purring reached my ears.

But I didn't share his content. I was hurt. I was hungry. Alone. And suddenly—more scared than I had ever been in my life.

"Grandmother?"

"Yes, child?"

"Were you very, very scared?"

"Yes, that night I was very, very scared."

Within the darkness, the girl looked at her panting mare, again lying upon the dried grasses near her feet. She studied the sweat-beaded face. Absently she lifted a palm to her own warm forehead. Then,

heaving a long, worried sigh, she nestled closer to
her grandmother's side and resumed twisting the
knotted button of her *del*.

"What did you do?" the girl said after a moment.
"I mean to say, you were lost and all alone in a dark
cave in the mountains. How did you keep from
screaming?"

A raspy chuckle rattled the old woman's chest.
"Well," she answered, "to tell truth, the screaming
came later. But that night, after I had done crying, and
still hugging my cat upon my lap, I tried very hard
to be cheerful." She paused, thinking. "You see, the
herdsman's life is not an easy one. Weather swings
from the heat of a fire to the cold of an ice storm, even
in the same day. Always moving the animals in
search of good grazing is difficult, and lonely. Sickness
and death arrive without warning." The wrinkle-
faced woman thought some more. "It is this way. When
you walk next to a great chasm all the time, you dare
not look down—only look to the sky with laughter."

She squeezed her granddaughter's arm. "But
laughter left with the next sun."

21. The Morning

*T*error. Absolute, flesh-chilling terror choked me with its bony fingers. For when morning's light first brushed my lids, I opened my eyes to look into dead, staring eyes. A gray hand stretched splintering claws toward my shoulder.

Again and again I screamed, until I thought my spirit would fly out of my mouth, leaving me lifeless within that stony grave. The shrill echoes banged around the damp walls like so many panic-stricken crows before fluttering into the cold mountain air.

Scrambling then, clawing the dirt, kicking at the saddle rug that suddenly entangled my legs, threatening to hold me captive, I fell back out of the cave. Kept pushing myself away from its dark mouth until I crouched, trembling, behind a massive boulder.

Panting, gasping—I couldn't breathe! My stomach was shoving aside my lungs. An unseen fist buried its punch into my middle and I doubled over, retching.

At the end I curled, weak and dampened, upon the

grainy earth, hardly noticing its wetness seeping through my clothing. Wrapping my arms around myself, I sobbed.

High on that mountaintop, my head brushing the heavens, I felt all had fallen away. I had nothing and no one, and death was reaching for me.

22. In the Grave of Echenkorlo

Sunshine buttered the mountaintop; a crisp breeze whistled through the pine boughs. Not more than an arrow's flight away, I could hear Bayan snuffling through the forest growth. Calling her name, I listened to the thin sound of my voice get swept up by the wind and empty into the skies. In a moment I saw the mud-spattered body of my white mare weaving a path through the trees. But when her front hoof clattered upon the shale outcropping leading up to the cave, she halted. Stretching her neck, Bayan sucked in the air through flaring pink nostrils. She snorted it out just as quickly, almost with alarm. A strong shudder began at her ears and rippled to her tail, spraying clots of dried mud upon the wet ground. Judgment passed, Bayan turned and walked into the woods.

She knew the death. She had, I realized, known it last night when she would not set a hoof inside the cave.

Chin upon my hands, I thought grimly how I, a dull human lacking basic animal senses, had passed one whole night practically nose to nose with death. It was my turn to shudder. There was no fleeing it this time. I had been caught. And I was unclean.

Into this cheerless morning flitted a faint tinkling sound, decidedly cheerful. Curious, I made a move to stand. But with the first gathering of limbs, my body crumpled back to the ground in sharp pain, the cries of my ribs and my bad foot rising above the others. As gently as possible, I pulled off the felt boot. Wincing, my fingers probed the hot flesh stretching across an ankle puffed twice its size. Lifting my trouser leg higher, I cringed at the sight of angry green and purple bruises splotching my skin. I sank back with a sigh. But a wrenching, ripping pain beneath my ribs caught me up short. I groaned, holding my hand to my side and bracing myself against the earth.

I was dying. I knew it. Having slept the night with a dead person, I was being dragged into the otherworld as well. I closed my eyes and waited.

Surely I dozed, for when I became uncomfortably aware of the sun hot upon my back I was still bracing myself on the ground. Maybe I wasn't dying, I thought, opening my eyes.

Having survived a sleep with death, could I be free of its curse? I had heard it told that in some parts of the land a powerful man might, upon his death, have his favorite servant buried with him—alive. Later, the dead man's friends come to dig up the grave and, if the servant is still breathing, great honor is laid upon his shoulders and he is set free to travel where he pleases. I had spent the night in a grave of sorts, I thought, and yet, here I was, squinting into the sunshine again.

Suddenly Bator was wedging his furry body beneath my arms to drop a dead field mouse in my lap. He set to shoving his bloody-whiskered face against my cheek again and again until I had to smile and lift a hand to stroke his back.

"Thank you, Bator," I murmured. Dangling the small rodent by its tail, I lied, "But I'm not very hungry. You take it." I flung the mouse into the air. Bator happily caught it between his paws before it hit the ground. I smiled again. "How would I ever get along without you?" I whispered.

There was a rustling behind me. Carefully peeking over my stiff shoulder, I saw Bayan poking her head curiously through some bare branches. "And you, too, Bayan," I said, laughing a little before a stitch in my ribs made me gasp.

Spying a branch dropped by the storm and lying crookedly not far from Bayan, I had an idea. Slithering across the ground like a half-witted snake, I managed to reach the branch, strip it of twigs, and prop it under one armpit. Then I draped my weight heavily across it and, lurching drunkenly, set off to investigate the tinkling sounds. Bator and Bayan, seemingly more curious about my sudden fifth limb than about the sounds, followed.

My breath was coming hard by the time I hobbled into a sunny clearing. Pointing to the heavens from its center was an *obo,* an impressive shrine to the mountain spirit created by travelers intertwining long tree branches into the form of a great cone. Numerous wet streamers of pale blue silk, knotted to these branches, fluttered limply. The silver beads of a broken necklace hung across one bough, twirling and blinking in the sunlight. And a rope of small brass bells bobbed in the spring breeze.

My father and I had passed just such an *obo* on our way to the festival at Karakorum. As then, I was awestruck.

Respectfully keeping the *obo* on my right, I hobbled a slow circle around it. Then I removed my belt, draped it around my neck, and, after bowing a painful nine times to the woody shrine, knelt upon the damp ground, eyes shut tightly. I fervently prayed to the mountain's spirit for protection. And for guidance.

In the darkness behind my closed lids, I sensed the earth quivering beneath my knees. A roaring, as of rushing water, filled my ears. A tremendous dizziness overcame me and I opened my eyes, flattening my palms against the earth to steady myself. But not before a thousand white horses, grinning crazily, filled my mind, leering and laughing in stiff silence. I vigorously shook my head clear of them.

I knew now why the shamans climbed so near the heavens for their visions. But I was no shaman, just a very tired, very hungry girl. I decided to return to the cave.

Pushing at the ground, dragging the crude crutch at my side, I began backing away from the *obo*. It was then that I noticed additional offerings to the mountain spirit on a nearby pile of flat-topped rocks. Trapped in a partially frozen puddle lay a few small coins and a broken piece of harness. A wet ring of hulls suggested an offering of grain, long since scattered by wind and birds. Upon another worn boulder an old wooden ladle held only a pale white skin of what must have once been *ayrag*. Beside it, glistening wet in the sunlight, sat a soaked block of tea leaves. So hungry was I that I let my fingers stretch out to touch its deep brown surface. My stomach growled, but I dared not steal food from the very bowl of the gods.

Remembering another offering I had seen at the *obo* with my father, I limped upon my stick to where Bayan grazed and plucked several hairs from her long white tail.

Then, though the dizziness was buzzing louder in my head, I made my way back to the *obo* and knotted them around one twig. Stepping back, satisfied, I watched the silky hairs drift in the breeze. My white mare always brought me luck. I would share it with the mountain spirit.

Already I began to feel stronger, more confident. The dizziness passed. And I began to think about the old person who had died in that desolate cave, alone and helpless. I wanted then to give the stranger some sort of burial so that the departed spirit would also find rest.

When I reentered the cave after another plodding trek upon my crutch, I saw something I had not noticed last evening: the feathery gray remains of a fire, with an object hard and white seated in its ashes. Even before my next step I recognized the shoulder blades of a sheep, seared so that the fire's maker could look into the future.

Smoky images swirled through my brain—images of Echenkorlo's tent, of her strange companion, of the oddly shaped fur bags strung in the haze. All at once I tasted again the musky brew, smelled the pungent herbs, saw the white-hot sheep's shoulders. In my mind, Udbal's toothless face hovered close to the crisscrossing lines, studying the future—my future. I shook my head clear once again. So the person inside had been a shaman . . . or a shamaness. My heart quickened. Could it be? No, it was impossible. The mountains were too many. More likely that the Golden Nail star would fall in with the Seven Giants than that Echenkorlo and I would be traveling the same path.

Still, with the hairs upon my arms stirring uneasily, I limped outside to look into the oxcart. Bundles of felt spilled from its end, as if someone had begun to set up a *ger,* then thought otherwise. Perhaps a sudden storm had chased the driver within the cave's shallow protection? But where was the ox? Something else was gnawing at the pit of my stomach. The felt for this *ger* was black, like Echenkorlo's. With both hands I dragged the heavy felt from the cart, its midnight color soaked with the warmth of the morning sun. I stared at what lay beneath: the strange pelts and furry pouches that I had seen in Echenkorlo's tent. So I *had* passed the night with my dead grandmother. Another shiver rippled my body. Suddenly I was very cold.

Out of respect for the dead, I swallowed my breath to tiptoe back inside the dark cave. Kneeling in the damp earth, I gazed down upon the cloudy eyes, the lipless yawning mouth. How had I not recognized that face—so powerful even in death? Even without Echenkorlo's mesmerizing words I was briefly held captive. Studying the wrinkles stacked one upon the other, I began to notice that a faint glow—like a late summer sky yet brushed golden by an unseen sun—caressed Echenkorlo's skin.

Frustration and sadness grew in my heart, spilling from my eyes in salty tears. Echenkorlo had started me on this journey, but the night she had leaned over my bed whispering words into my ear seemed ages ago. I could not remember half of what she had taught me. And now I would never know. I realized with a start then that I, Oyuna of the Kerait tribe, still less than thirteen springs, was now the oldest female member of my family. A heavy responsibility, born of generations of caring for the living and the dead, settled upon my shoulders. Although tears continued trickling down my cheeks, I set about doing what I had to do.

Gritting my teeth, I dug my hands into the unfeeling armpits and tugged, finally managing to drag the stiff body to the small back of the cave. There was no odor. The cold mountain air had frozen the flesh. At first I placed my grandmother upon her back, as was proper, but after fighting unsuccessfully with her rigid, outstretched arm, I rolled her onto one side, so that she slept with her head resting upon the unyielding limb. Then by gentle nudges, I wedged her body into the protective crevice of the cave's back. Carrying the brown woven blanket that had been crumpled beside her into the fresh air, I shook it free of dirt. Something flew from its folds. My eyes followed the thumb-sized object sliding upon the shale until it came to a stop, shimmering dully in the sunlight.

Bending over stiffly, I saw that it was the same black amulet that had magically appeared in Echenkorlo's palm that night long ago. The small figure upon the galloping horse so closely resembled the gold ornament I carried in my pocket that I pulled it forth to compare. Studying them in the bright light, I was certain that both craftings must have come from the hands of the same artist. Only in the larger one, the ornament, did the horse sprout wings and you could see that the rider was a girl carrying flowers in her hands. I let my fingers close around the black amulet as I remembered Echenkorlo's words. "Can you not reach out and take either good luck or bad luck into your hand?" One by one, I unfolded my fingers, but the black charm was still there. Echenkorlo's tricks would forever remain her secret. Smiling a little, I slipped the ornament inside my pocket and carried the amulet and the blanket back inside the cave.

I fit the amulet inside the leathery palm Echenkorlo curled toward her body, then covered her from head to toe in the brown blanket. In rummaging through her cart I had found a food bowl, which I placed beside her head.

Still I frowned. What would my grandmother have to eat in the next world? I had no milk to pour into her bowl, nor any mare with a foal. Returning to her cart yet again, I began yanking open the necks of the many leather bags. At the start I found only lots of roots, herbs, and powders, but when I lifted a particularly heavy goatskin bag to my lap, my hands plunged into an oily abundance of dried meat strips. I must admit that the first one I stuffed straight into my mouth, my tongue bursting wet at the taste. Then I carried a fistful of strips inside and tucked them inside Echenkorlo's *del.* We both felt better. For now I had food in my mouth, and she would always have food at hand.

As I gazed at the wrinkled face I wondered if my grandmother had died alone. Had Udbal held her hand until the end or had they parted paths long ago? I looked at the plain clothing, remembering how different—how elegant—my mother had looked on the day of her burial. But Echenkorlo owned no finely embroided *dels,* no glittering jewelry. Although she had gathered a great number of oddities in her travels, wealth was not among them. Still, I wanted to send her into the next world with something more. Recalling the delicate white flowers I had noticed blooming in a rocky crevice, I hobbled from the cave and returned clutching a spring bouquet, which I nestled beneath her nostrils. Whatever the next world held, I thought, my grandmother would always carry with her the fragrance of this one.

Then I busied myself stacking around her the furry bags and leather pouches holding the remedies for untold ills, so that she might continue her healing ways in the otherworld. I confidently identified the contents of only four bags and scooped a few handfuls of each for my own use.

During one of the many trips I made between the cart and the cave, and in the muddy area where I had first found my grandmother, I noticed a handprint, though my careless footprints had nearly obscured it. Dropping the armful of pouches I was carrying, I knelt beside it. Gently I brushed away the grit that had been knocked across the impression by my coming and going.

So my grandmother had been able to foretell her own death, I thought, for I was not unfamiliar with the burial practice of pressing a dead person's hand into the wet earth inside a grave. Then I noticed more impressions. Bending close to the ground, straining in the dim light of the cave, I made out a finger-drawn design of a long-rooted flower. Beside it was the stiff stick figure of a horse wearing a sickly grin. The roaring sound that had filled my ears near the *obo* again rushed through me, leaving me dizzy and weakened. What did it mean? I dug my nails into the wet earth and forced myself to study the third drawing: an oblong shape patterned very much like the Khan's *paiza* I had left behind. For many long, calming breaths I huddled over these images, but my mind could pull no message from them.

Shaking my head as I rose, I finished piling the pouches around Echenkorlo. Then I left the cave, hunted for a stone I could lift, and began a morning of nonstop circling. With each coming I pressed a stone or a branch against the stiff body of my grandmother; with each going I limped, empty-handed, in search of another burial offering. These trips were not easy, for my leg throbbed with pain and I had to balance each weighty load on the hip away from my tender ribs. All the while Bator scampered about, at one point catching and devouring a small bird. I didn't see Bayan, although when I paused to cock an ear I was certain I heard her hooves slopping through the mud.

The sun was already sliding past its highest point and I was sweating lightly, even in the cold mountain air, when I wedged the last small stone into the makeshift wall. Exhausted, I stumbled outside to rest upon the empty oxcart. Hands dirty and scraped lifted strips of dried meat to my own panting mouth, tossed smaller bits toward the meowing pink mouth of Bator. Intermingled with the wind and the tinkling I could once again make out the babble of the mountain stream. The sound awakened in me the urge to move on. I wondered briefly if I could hitch Bayan to the oxcart, for the harness lay empty before it. But as the mare wandered into view, dyed nearly brown from a good roll in the mud, I decided we could make faster time if I continued to ride her.

I called to Bayan. This time when she sniffed the air she seemed satisfied and sauntered toward the oxcart. Bator arched his back in greeting and the mare ruffled his fur with her lips. Laughing to myself, and feeling strangely renewed, I hobbled to the cave to gather up my things.

The white shoulder blades of the sheep were still sitting starkly among the cold ashes of the long-dead fire. Idly curious, I paused to stoop over them a last time, boldly attempting to understand the webwork as Echenkorlo and Udbal had done. From that mysterious night long ago I could remember only which lines referred to journeys, so I turned over the blades and studied the thin cracks.

The angle of the lines at first seemed to suggest a dangerous journey, but then they faded in such a way as to make it impossible to determine their message. I rocked back upon my haunches, thinking. Had Echenkorlo been trying to foretell her own journey? Was she trapped upon the mountain and wondering if she would escape? Or was she probing the outcome of a future journey, one not yet begun?

I shrugged. Gingerly carrying the shoulder blades to the back of the cave, I set them against the slanting wall. The lines meant something to Echenkorlo, perhaps, but not to me.

Emerging into the sunlight, I found a width of bark and scraped the drying mud from Bayan's back as best I could. Then I saddled and bridled her, heaved the Khan's mysterious, heavy bags across, and climbed up. Tipping my head to listen, I reined Bayan toward the rippling stream and, I hoped, our path out of the mountains. Bator picked his way behind us.

23. A Gobi

*N*o one had told me how far it was to Khanbaliq! Thoughts of bad luck and my grandmother's death had to be pushed aside as I struggled just to survive each long day.

The land around us was changing. We had left the mountains at our backs and the grassy steppes once again sprawled in great rolling waves in every direction, much like my homeland. Yet more and more often Bayan's hooves clip-clopped across hard spots of bare earth, littered with blowing sand and jutting rocks.

We had fallen upon a caravan route, its faint and many-fingered path worn into the dirt by hundreds of years and thousands of feet. I rode openly as a girl now and, although this was quite uncommon, I felt fairly safe. My people always welcome strangers and it was widely boasted at that time that a young woman—if she had wanted—could walk across the lands of Kublai Khan carrying a pot of gold on her head and not be bothered. But that didn't stop people from staring.

About every other day our trio rode up on a small mud-walled shelter, usually near water rising from a well or spring. These dwellings served as arrow stations, with ten or twelve scrawny replacement horses always hobbled nearby. Caravans traveling between markets also stopped to water their animals and exchange news with the station's keeper. I was grateful when a box of mud rose into view quiet and empty, for this meant I could water Bayan, fill my pouch, and ride on without explanation. When a caravan was resting—camels and oxen kneeling like so many hairy hillocks upon the steppe—my arrival would cause a great waving of arms and shouted invitations to sit. A girl, riding alone and carrying a cat, they figured, must also be carrying a story, and the drivers and their families always hungered for stories.

I spoke shyly, answering questions as they were asked. The men, and some of the women, snorted at my talk of riding straight into Kublai Khan's royal courtyard. "You should stay within your *ger* with a husband," the fathers scolded. "Or at least with your family," the women chided. But in the dust-filled eyes of some of the women, especially the girls, I saw a small spark of envy.

Of course I did not tell everything—especially not about Bayan sometimes talking to me or about the dreams that had been troubling me. Almost nightly since leaving the mountain, my sleep had been broken by the ghostly images of white horses, their faces contorted in silent laughter. I had begun to dread the daily sinking of the sun, for I did not understand what I had done to bring such torment upon myself.

With each day's travel southward, the steppe withered. The grasses dwindled to a few gray-green weeds choking between cracked plates of baked earth. The air hung motionless and hot, and no matter how steadily we trod toward it, the horizon seemed to hover, shimmering, ever out of reach. So this was a *gobi*.

Although the ground stretched flatly ahead of us, inviting speed, I could not cross it any faster than if it had been mountains, for the injuries I had suffered were still healing. Any gait more than a walk remained unbearably painful. Yet, while I sensed my own body healing, I watched Bayan's body grow stiffer and weaker with each day's trek. When we would finally halt at midmorning to wait out the sun's heat, the old mare would drop to her knees as soon as I unsaddled her. She would settle there all day, not even rising to graze, though her ears pricked steadily southward. Gradually heat and exhaustion would coax her muzzle downward, as she drowsed, into the shadows of her neck, and she would rest. Worry ate at me. Steppe horses are known for their sturdy nature, able to live through the harshest conditions on little food. But, looking around, I saw the *gobi* held hardly anything at all for Bayan. Her teeth had to strip bark from tiny-leaved bushes and her sharp hooves had to unearth pale bulbs. With each day her hide stretched more tightly across jutting wither and hip.

Water, too, became scarce, especially when we didn't come upon an arrow station before we stopped for the heat of the day. In the early morning hours I tried very hard to "smell" water as I had on the way from Karakorum. But with the *gobi*'s dust coating my eyes, nose, and throat, I could smell nothing. So I trusted Bayan to find water, urging her with a free rein and repeating the word, "*Usan! Usan!*" But even her senses seemed dulled.

Luckily, before long, my eyes grew well attuned to spotting wild camels and *kulans* from afar and following them—at a safe distance, for this was springtime and the bulls and stallions were territorial—to watering holes. Little more than muddy ponds, they grew thick with yellow rushes and rippled with the splashes of wading birds and black-headed ducks. Invariably the water was warm and lay stale upon the tongue, yet the three of us bent our heads and drank gratefully. Then we retreated a distance and collapsed beneath the blistering sun.

Bator always stretched, eyes closed and pink tongue fluttering, in the speckled shelter of some small bush. I hid my face within the hot shade offered by the upturned saddle and tried not to think about the rivulets of sweat running down my neck, under my armpits, between my legs. The padded winter *del* of my stepbrother, lined with sheepskin, sagged heavily upon my damp body. I welcomed its thickness in the night's piercing cold, but in the day—how I longed to strip it from my body! We passed the day, then, half-waking, just waiting and waiting for an end to the burning heat. In the vast *gobi* it was too hot to move, too hot to eat, too hot even to think.

Not until after the sun had dropped below the horizon were we able to sleep comfortably. We awoke to the cool light of the moon probing our eyelids and the chill night air brushing our cheeks. Always I took immediate notice of the moon—whether it was shrinking or swelling—for in the past two months, I had begun to feel its pull upon my own body. With a long groan Bayan would lunge stiffly to her feet, shake off the dust, and, nose to the ground, wander off in search of grazing. My worried eyes followed her into the darkness.

Bator worried me, too, for each night he seemed to leap to his feet with added restlessness. Instead of curling beside me, round eyes intently watching as I sparked a fire with my steel, the little cat took to pacing in wide circles, crying to the moon. The wailing grew fainter as the circles grew larger. One night, after Bator had left the fire, I heard a feline scream in the distance that chased tight bumps up my arms. I stood, holding my breath, but then nothing more. A short while later, though, I looked up to see two round yellow eyes watching me. In the next instant a smaller pair of yellow-green eyes stared across the fire. Unmoving, the animals watched each other for a long, long time, neither making a sound. Then the one with the yellow-green eyes edged closer to the fire. It was Bator! He came slinking, his fur stiff upon his back, to sit, tail switching, beside me. When I looked up, the other animal was gone.

My one daily meal was taken after dark and began with tea boiled in the small iron cooking pot Echenkorlo had given me. When I had drunk the tea, I would dig through the pouch and toss into the pot any bits of meat I had been kindly handed by other travelers. When my hands came up empty one evening, my stomach growled an instant complaint. Bator had always been good about sharing his catches, but game was as scarce as grass in the *gobi,* resulting in only two gray-green lizards, which I had, with a grimace, thrown back to the waiting cat.

And so that night I caught, cooked, and ate my first fish, though my tongue still twists at the memory. Pulling from the pouch the fishhook and line Echenkorlo had given me, I snatched a large moth that had been flitting in and out of the firelight and pressed its fluttering body onto the prong. Then I marched down to the moonlit pond and, after rippling its surface with my bait for just a few moments, yanked a small fish, flopping, onto the shore. I dug out the fish's purple and orange insides with my knife and threw what was left into the pot of boiling water. The cooked flesh was mushy and tasteless, but my stomach stopped growling and I rested beside the fire rather proud of my newfound skill.

I always ended up fingering the wax-sealed knot tying the Khan's bags and wondering what they hid. I thought I could feel sharp points of dried grasses poking at the goatskin that protected what nestled inside. Porcelain tea bowls like the ones Genma collected? Gold icons for a temple? Jewel-encrusted bridles and breast collars?

On another night, with the cooking pot already stowed and a bright half-moon floating overhead, I was just setting the saddle upon Bayan's back when an animal's shrill squeal made me jump almost out of my skin. Spinning around, I came face to face with the head-tossing, yellow-coated body of a wild *gobi* stallion. In the darkness behind him, ears pricked with interest, huddled his herd of timid mares. And among the striped legs and stiff black manes cowered several steppe ponies like Bayan!

The heavy-headed stallion pawed the dirt and lifted his chalky mouth in another piercing squeal. Suddenly, teeth bared, he charged, knocking me to the ground as he bit and kicked at Bayan, trying to drive her into his herd. With the force of his attack, the saddle slid away. But the reins were wrapped around my fist and Bayan, thus tethered to my weight, could only dance in a circle, trying to avoid the cruel blows while trying not to trample me. I scrambled to my feet. The stallion charged again, ramming Bayan with his shoulder as he tore at her neck and bellowed. It was my turn to dance out of the way, yanking on the reins to swing Bayan around behind me. The stallion shook his head angrily. Black eyes on fire, he stared right through me at Bayan. Pawing the ground, he prepared another charge. I threw up my hands, stamped my feet, and yelled with all my might. He swung away, half-startled, as if seeing me for the first time. Snorting loudly, the sand-colored animal sucked in the cold air again and again, trying to decide how dangerous I might be. His sides shuddered like a door flap in the wind. When one of the mares behind him nickered, he flicked an ear backward. Then, with a rumble that began deep inside him and burst forth in a chilling scream, the wild stallion charged again. His weight pinned me against Bayan's shoulder until she stumbled backward. I felt the reins ripped from my hands as I slipped to the ground, the air knocked from my chest. In an instant, hundreds of hooves were pounding the earth, stirring up a pale dust that hung in the air like a choking fog. Gradually the thunder faded and the silence of the night closed in around me.

My fingers pulled at the sand, but the grains sifted through them and fell away. Blindly I stared upward, head throbbing, my addled brain screaming at my body to do something, do something! Gradually I became aware of my trembling arms lifting my weight from the dirt. Yet I remained slumped against one arm, gasping for air and shaking all over. A terror I kept trying to push aside— being stranded alone and on foot in this *gobi*—clamped down upon my mind like a dog's teeth upon the neck of its kill.

My ears caught the sound of the galloping hooves again; groggily I scrambled to my feet. There weren't as many this time. I could not see a thing in the dust-filled air, but I could tell the hooves were headed my way. I had no place to run. Then, like a spirit careering out of the afterlife, the white body of a horse crashed through the silty fog and came to a halt at my side. Bayan! She was back!

Panting heavily, my white mare kept rolling her eyes nervously as she pranced fitfully in tight circles around me. She kept looking into the darkness. We both listened, but caught no echoing sound of hooves. I rested a hand upon Bayan's withers, wet with the stallion's bites, and stroked her neck, trying to calm her. I tipped my head into the darkness for just another breath or two before deciding we had better use this chance to escape.

It was a struggle to fasten the saddle upon Bayan's shifting back. But I managed to tighten it, then to lift the Khan's bags across the seat, though they thumped against the mare's sides as she continued pacing restlessly around me. I hadn't seen any bloody wounds from her attack, but I did notice that one of her reins had been torn from the bit. Ripping three strips of silk from the belt around my waist, I quickly braided them into a strong cord and tied one end to the bit. Then I climbed into the saddle, Bayan practically bolting from beneath me in a lunge toward the south's shadowy horizon.

"Bator!" I called as we trotted off. "Bator!"

From out of the cloudy night leaped a tiger-striped bundle of fur, claws digging painfully into my trousers for a hold. The terrified look on his face must have mirrored my own. I reached down to scoop up the panting cat, pulling him securely into my lap. Then I gave Bayan her head. The three of us were off.

With a groan long and low, the stiff-boned woman struggled to her feet. Leaning against the splintered stable wall for a breath to gain her balance, she saw the look of alarm flash across her granddaughter's face.

"Do not worry yourself. Both your mare and I are fine."

She limped the short distance to where the white

head stretched from a quivering neck. Bending ever
so slowly, the woman placed her gnarled hand upon
the flat brow. She listened. Then, still in silence,
she tapped the jade pendant knotted around the mare's
throat—once, twice—and stepped past the white
belly rising and falling in straining rhythm. Echoing
her earlier groan, the old woman sank into the dried
grasses.

"I have no idea how Bayan got away from the *gobi*
stallion that night," she was saying as her hands smoothed
the trembling flank. "But every evening after that I
remembered to paint blood upon her forehead before
she moved off to graze. For protection," she finished.

The age-darkened hands lifted the silky white tail
hairs and began nimbly braiding.

"What are you doing?" asked the girl, sitting upon
her knees. "Are you sure she's all right?"

"Yes, yes," soothed the wise voice. "The time is
coming. Be still and listen."

24. Ice-fire, Earth Serpents, and the Jade Green Eyes

*W*hen we had plodded the *gobi* a very long time, the land changed again. The sandy, gravelly earth gave way to rolling green hills that splashed skyward into distant blue mountains. Our path twisted through them. The instant we leaned our backs into the climb, shadows cool and wet began fingering our shoulders and fitful breezes whispered imperfect directions. As firmly as the hairs rose upon my arms I knew we had entered a strange place.

The land's dangers tested our courage one dusky evening when a thick fog crept silently behind us, then billowed past, hiding the narrow path. Bayan, Bator, and I were forced to doze in our tracks, huddled hard beside a cold mountain wall. All through that blinded night I clutched a rocky crevice with one hand, my lucky gold ornament with the other, so fearful was I of falling over into the dark chasm below.

But when we awoke—such a sight! Every rocky dimple, every peeling twig, every tiny leaf had been painted a glittering silver. And towering directly above us in the sparkling morning air was a magnificent white palace, roof upon roof swooping across the sky like the upturned wings of so many birds. We had truly entered a magical land, I remember thinking, for only a god could have built upon the crests of mountains. At that moment an orange sun burst between the peaks, setting flashing fire to each crystal droplet. I knew not which gods lived in these mountains, but I quickly bowed my head nine times toward the palace, clutched the luck within my pocket close to my side, and, tugging on Bayan's reins, scurried on along the path.

The few faces I began to meet also changed, becoming flatter. These persons stared at me, not with the kindness of my own people, but with distrust, and then, when they realized that behind the dirty face was only a girl, with annoyance.

"*Sain bainu?*" I always called politely. But they pretended not to understand me. "Which direction to the Khan?" I would ask. Yet their mouths hung open, their eyes blinked dully. Sometimes a torrent of cackling sounds would ripple past my ears without giving up their meaning. Then we could only stare at each other until Bayan stamped an impatient hoof and we rode away.

But soon I grew skilled at using my hands and eyes to make my needs understood. Even though the people I met remained grim and unsmiling, I gestured on. Pointing to the waxen knots upon the twin bags, each stamped with the royal seal, I spoke the words "Kublai Khan?" and, with an upturned palm scanning the horizon, raised my eyebrows. Without fail, at least one person would point to a hill or a notch upon the next horizon. Nodding my thanks, I would rein Bayan into line with the outstretched finger. In this way we continued our journey to deliver the Khan's treasure and to find my swift horse.

We padded through lush valleys, Bayan, Bator, and I, our heads now shaded by gently drooping, long-leaved trees. My eyes, and those of Bayan, too, I think, looked upon the rich green grasses as heavenly fare for horses. Yet we saw few such creatures. And the people we passed did not gallop proudly upon their horses' backs, but hunched, half-naked, over muddy ditches dug into the land. At day's end, we watched them shuffle behind the mud walls surrounding their dark homes, pulling in after them the caged larks that hung by each doorway.

Sometimes I wanted to shout at them to get up from the ground, to climb upon the back of a horse and feel the wind ripping through their lungs. But in the end I rode past the earth-workers without speaking, only feeling a stinging sorrow for them.

Hunger was gnawing at me again. The camel's milk I had been given by some traders at the *gobi*'s edge was long gone. I should not have been surprised that the people I passed did not offer me food or drink, for they rarely even lifted a head at my approach. In my land one never lets a stranger pass without inviting him into one's *ger*. To do otherwise would be rude. But in this odd land, not once was I offered a morsel. Even when, in hungry desperation, I pointed to my open mouth and rubbed my stomach, I received only a grunt and a wave of the hand. To this day I thank Tengri for my cunning cat, Bator. For each evening as I unsaddled Bayan, Bator would disappear into the darkness, almost always returning with some small furred animal hanging limply from his mouth.

One day I was riding past gray earthen walls enclosing more mud homes when a woman strode toward me, cackling and pointing. I reined Bayan to a halt. Terrified, Bator leaped from the saddle and hid among the drooping fronds of a creek-side tree. The woman cackled some more, her dirty finger pointing at my knee. I realized then she was pointing to one of the silver ornaments sewn onto Genma's saddle. I realized, too, that I could probably fill my stomach by making a trade. In pointing my own finger toward the silver medallion, then to her, then to my mouth, I set the woman's head to nodding vigorously. She turned back inside the mud walls, then returned carrying a small cloth sack and a large knife. Handing me the sack, which weighed in my palm as grain, the woman cut the medallion free in one stroke. We each parted happily.

That evening I boiled a handful of the grain in my iron pot and discovered that the result, though sticky, bore a pleasant nutty flavor. I saddled Bayan the next morning already looking forward to my one meal. Bator continued to hunt and so twice I had blackened bits of meat to add to my bowl.

When we had traveled eight more days, the saddle had grown plainer, but my pouch fairly bulged with grains, fruits, and the eggs of birds. To tell truth, I could not stomach the idea of swallowing the slippery yolks, so I broke the shells into the dirt and let Bator lap up the yellow ooze.

We were climbing down from another string of small mountains, careful on the pebble-strewn path, when we saw the long ragged backbone of some gigantic snake or lizard slumping across the valley below and disappearing over the backs of the distant hills. I reined Bayan to a sliding stop with my jaw dropped. Only after several blinking moments did I realize that the winding, earth-colored ridge was an endless mud wall that traveled in opposite directions farther than my eyes could see. This, too, must have been thrown up by the gods, for how could any man have built a wall that had no end?

By late afternoon, the sun hanging low in a pink sky, Bayan, Bator, and I cautiously approached the rambling creation that rose past our heads. We could now see that the ancient wall was crumbling in many places and that no soldiers guarded it. Still, my heart beat fast as Bayan picked a passage around the rubble and we crossed through this eerie barrier.

In the shadows of the long wall shrank another cluster of mud homes. I saw one of the earth-workers slip within an open doorway that faced me, so, riding up to it, I called a greeting. A raggedly dressed girl not much older than me appeared in the door frame, jostling a wailing child upon her hip. I pointed at one of the few ornaments left sewn to the saddle, yet, with no more than a quick scowl, the agitated mother dismissed me. I reined Bayan back to the path. But a loud hissing sound made me look over my shoulder.

A frail-looking woman wrapped in lavender gray was leaning against the door frame and motioning for me to return. Obviously curious, I circled back. When the woman remained fastened to the door frame, I dismounted and hobbled within a respectful distance. Bator had hopped from the saddle with me, but stayed seated beside Bayan's hooves. The slender hand motioned me still closer. More than a little nervous, I moved near enough to smell the woman's oniony breath. She wasn't old, although her face looked tired, even sickly. But it was her eyes that held my attention—twin cloudy green moons flecked with gold. And they stared into the last rays of the sun without blinking.

So mesmerized was I that I did not notice the trembling hand reaching for my chest until I felt the bony fingers probing my *del*. They searched for, and found, the jade horse pendant I wore hidden next to my skin. Smiling secretively, the fragile woman tapped the pendant twice, then raised her hand to my head. Still she said nothing. Placing her cool, smooth palm firmly against my forehead, she turned her gaze to mine. For the several long breaths we stood face-to-face, I wondered what, if anything, her clouded eyes were seeing. But I had no answer. At last the woman smiled and nodded, dropping her hand.

In the wavering motion of ill health, she bent over to drag several bags from behind her into the dirt outside the doorway. Her hands fluttered, urging me to take the bags. It was almost as if she had been waiting with them, knowing that I was coming. Nodding in acceptance, I clutched two bags in each fist and set them at my feet.

Looking up then, I saw the slight woman silently pointing a finger at the leather pouch given to me by Echenkorlo and strung across my chest. Somehow I trusted her and, also without speaking, lifted the pouch from my shoulder and opened wide its neck between us. With a whistling sound, like that of a bird, the woman excitedly scooped her hands inside the pouch and pulled forth the small bags containing the dried herbs I had taken from Echenkorlo's possessions the night I buried her. One after the other she lifted them to her nose, each deep inhalation blossoming into a radiant smile. Nodding and gesturing then, the woman seemed to be asking if she might take some of the herbs for herself. I eyed the four heavy bags lying at my feet and nodded agreement. When she kept bobbing her head excitedly, I placed one hand over hers and squeezed. Immediately the woman's smile widened into a satisfied grin. Stooping over, she pulled several large pieces of silk from a pocket, spread them upon the dirt, and scooped a small handful of each herb into each square. She quickly knotted them, then dropped the silken bags back inside her pocket.

"You come our land." The woman's crackly words were haltingly spoken in my own tongue! "Danger come also. Hear the mare."

The complaining voice of the young mother rose above her child's wail and with a last warning—"Go! Now!"— the frail woman sank into the room's shadows. Quickly I climbed into Bayan's saddle, Bator leaped onto my lap, and with eyes darting this way and that across the horizon, we rode long after the sun had set. Not until many more hills rose and fell at our backs did we stop to hide behind a curtain of drooping tree fronds.

In the darkness of evening and the tree's shadows, I peered into the sacks offered by the cloudy-eyed woman and found, mostly through touch and smell, some of the favorite foods of my homeland: *aaruul,* dried mutton, powdered mare's milk, and a block of tea leaves. Yet so nervous was my stomach that I could only hold a salty-sweet piece of *aaruul* upon my tongue and lie, ears cocked for danger, until I fell asleep.

The muffled sound of gentle rain awakened me. At my first stirring, Bator meowed sleepily and pushed his feet against my stomach in protest. Rolling over anyway, I saw that Bayan was still kneeling within the tree's thick shelter, though her black eyes looked at me with alert interest. Remembering the danger that followed us, I set about saddling Bayan so that we could be on our way. Bator pouted and switched his tail.

The fine, continuous rain followed us all morning as

we rode past first one and then another cluster of mud-walled homes, their occupants already outside and bending over the endless rows of black ditches. Close to midday, however, a wind blew from the west, chasing away the clouds to reveal a clear sky the deep blue of sapphires. It was with the sun shining upon a freshly scrubbed land neatly embroidered into great squares of yellow and green and black that we came upon another of the gods' wonders.

At the bank of a wide, slow-moving river, our path leaped into the air and landed upon the other side in a great arching of gleaming white stone. Enormous slabs, carved and smoothed, rested upon gigantic columns that rose magically from the murky brown water. People from both directions were indifferently lifting their heels from the land and walking confidently upon these slabs suspended high above the river.

Bayan snorted and lowered her head. I did not know whether to urge her on or rein her back. Tentatively she placed a hoof upon the rock pathway. It didn't slip off. She placed another hoof upon the slab and snorted again. Then another hoof and another and we were walking through the air.

My heart was thundering in my ears so loudly that I never heard them coming. With both hands I was clutching the arching front of the saddle, fearful that I would tumble off and into the river below, and fervently staring at the solid ground ahead. Bator was hunkered almost flat against my lap, hiding his face in my *del*. With one cautious step after another, Bayan crossed over the river and kept us all dry. The instant she set a hoof upon the opposite bank, though, a man's stern voice spoke in the tongue of my people: "What are you carrying?"

Stunned, I looked up to see a soldier splendidly dressed

in black mounted upon a fine dark horse outfitted with a red bridle and blanket. I began to smile, but the man's hard face, lined like the cracked boulders of the mountains we had passed through, chased it away.

I sat tall. "I am a messenger of the Khan," I said proudly, pointing to the seals upon the bags.

"Show me your *paiza*," the soldier commanded.

My face flushed hot. I looked down at my hands. "I . . . I lost it," I lied.

"You are a thief!" the man shouted. "You must come with us."

In an instant, soldiers—all dressed in black and riding black horses—swept around us like a torrent of rushing water, crowding Bayan tightly. She pinned back her ears and snapped at a bold gelding who likewise flattened his ears and shook his head angrily. Another horse reached out to bite Bayan's flank. She squealed and arched her back to kick, but the wave was rolling forward, carrying us with it. We galloped, pulled deeper and deeper into this strange land as helplessly as a pale leaf in a muddy current.

25. At the Court of Kublai Khan

They took everything. Everything!

Before we galloped, the soldiers' leader had lifted the twin goatskin bags and draped them across his own saddle. By his order another soldier had torn Echenkorlo's pouch from my neck. His groping hands then dug inside my *del*, pulling a frantically clawing Bator by his tail into the sunlight. The mean-spirited man had held my poor cat upside down in the air and laughed while Bator hissed and screamed.

"Stop! Stop!" I yelled. But my voice was drowned in the coarse laughter of the surrounding soldiers. Bator must have managed to swipe his claws across his tormentor's exposed wrist, for, with a snarling curse, the man slammed him to the ground and lifted the bloodied arm to his mouth. With tear-filled eyes I watched the terrified cat, my faithful friend, tear through the forest of hooves and out of my sight.

But already this horrid soldier was back, his hands digging through my *del* again. Bayan squealed. In a flash her head snaked out, teeth bared, and snapped at the soldier's rangy horse. She spun and kicked. I heard bone crack. The big horse shrank back, but the soldier mercilessly spurred him forward, charging against Bayan's shoulder so hard that we almost toppled over. His hairy hand found the winged horse ornament hidden deep within my pocket. With a chortle, he pulled it into the light.

But there was no time for examining the gold trophy, for his leader snatched it from his raised hand and called for the gallop. Still searching over my shoulder for a glimpse of poor Bator, I was swept along toward Khanbaliq, "City of the Khan." For more than a moon I had pictured my triumphant entry into the royal city. Now I entered it a criminal.

Riding with a heavy heart, I paid little attention to the sights that would otherwise have thrilled me. I do remember our path was thick with people, even more than I had seen at Karakorum. We rode through markets crowded with sellers and buyers, animals and cooks, sharp smells and loud sounds. Then the high walls of the great city, straight as an arrow's flight, stretched before us farther than I could see. Calls of greeting met the leader as most of the soldiers split away, leaving only half a dozen to escort their prisoner through a series of huge, heavily guarded gates.

At last we passed into the city, center of Kublai Khan's vast empire. All was noise, color, and wealth. Under one roof tumbled a pile of saddles, men bent over them hammering upon gold and silver ornaments. Under another spilled thousands upon thousands of bows and arrows. Sweating, bare-backed men pulled great swaths of leather from boiling pots; others bent over fiery hot metal, pounding it into sharp points. Each of the roofs was painted a different brilliant color—red, green, blue, yellow—and polished so that it looked wet and shining in the sun.

With nods exchanged between soldiers, we passed through another gate and, I guessed, onto the palace grounds, for the scene that stretched before me was so astonishing as to dry the tears from my swollen eyes. A winding walkway floated above grasses alive with wild animals that didn't run from us in fear: white stags, roe deer and fallow deer, squirrels and ermines. Behind them rose an immense green hill that magically sprouted trees of all kinds. A great commotion was taking place near the far slope. My eyes widened in fear and I shrank in the saddle, for monstrous gray and hairless animals—which I later came to know as elephants—were carrying whole trees in their long snouts, expertly setting them into holes at the direction of dark-skinned herdsmen.

At the next gateway we halted and I was ordered off Bayan. Looking into the black eyes that calmly stared back at me, I threw my arms around her neck: I did not know if I would ever see her again. Surrounded by armored soldiers then, I marched into the palace. In front of me the soldiers' leader carried across his shoulders the leather pouch Echenkorlo had given me as well as the twin goatskin bags I had worked so hard to deliver. Without words we marched through room after room until I was hopelessly lost. Between the thick arms and hunched shoulders jostling me, I caught glimpses of beautifully painted walls—gold and silver and blue—each ornamented with long-tailed birds and great lizards breathing fire.

We stopped again as the soldiers, braced against the bent backs of pretty palace women, pulled off their dirty boots and replaced them with soft leather slippers. I, too, traded my felt boots for white slippers. We waited while the leader passed through the doorway ahead of us. None of the men spoke, although the women stood whispering and looking at me curiously.

When the leader returned, he ripped the slippers from his feet and spat curses from his lips. He ordered the soldiers to replace their boots. Immediately I sat upon the floor and began removing my slippers, but was yanked to my feet by the leader's iron grip.

"The Khan will speak with you." He shoved me, all alone, through the doorway.

Near to fainting, I tiptoed down a long cool hall, its pale blue ceiling arching above my head as high as the sky itself. Stone columns the size of tree trunks, polished smooth as water, marched at my side. The air was still, yet I caught the sweet smell of steppe grasses. Strange, I thought. Before I had done gathering my courage, I reached the end of the hallway. Holding my breath, I peeked around the corner, not knowing what the fearsome Khan would look like. Or what he would do to me.

At the far side of a huge room, its gleaming stone floor strewn with *shirdiks* thickly woven and richly colored, sat a fat, balding man. But not in the golden seat of honor, empty at the top of a mountain of stairs. This man reclined, knees lazily spread, upon a wide bottom step between the two goatskin bags—the seals of which he was studying. He was old, a grandfather many times over, and draped in an especially fine silk *del* the color of snow. I noticed that his small feet were not covered in felt boots or leather slippers but loosely wrapped in the soft skins of some unknown animal. Bare ankles poked from the skins.

The man noticed me and lifted his arm. "Enter, enter." He, too, spoke in the language of my people and I grew certain this was the great Kublai Khan, for he, like his grandfather Genghis before him, was born upon the steppes.

Heart in my throat, I nervously began covering the padded distance between us. Each slippered footfall upon the thick *shirdiks* breathed a sigh and fell silent.

Just as I neared the man, a snarling leopard sprang at me from behind a large table. I was to be killed, I thought in a flash. This was a trap. Dropping to my knees, I covered my head with my arms. But before the large spotted cat could rip me apart, a chain attached to a collar around its neck yanked it to a hissing stop.

"Cease. All is well. At least for now." Trembling, I looked up. The words were being spoken to the leopard, not to me. "This girl will explain her arrival and then we will decide how you eat." The leopard flung its body onto a pile of dried grasses, stirring the scent of the steppes into the air, and fixed its green eyes upon me. "We thought they had been lost. How did you come to carry them here?"

With a start I realized these last words were directed at me. Scrambling to my feet, I tried to bring a response into my mouth. But I found myself speechless before the most powerful man in this world. I was certain he had killed thousands of people for lesser slights than not speaking when so ordered, yet all I could do was stare—at the white powder covering his face, just like a woman! The makeup blanched his skin, though his cheeks glowed as pink as tulips. A silky white mustache drooped over a sparse, combed-clean beard. From beneath the limp head covering, which slipped sideways, I saw thin gray hair coiled into braided loops.

Impatient, the Khan posed another question. "Where is my gold *paiza?*"

"I forgot it," I mumbled.

"You stole it!"

"I did not!" I cried too loudly. The leopard growled and shifted its haunches.

The Khan grasped the sealed neck of each bag in a fist. "You were caught riding away with these bags but not the gold *paiza*."

"I wasn't riding away," I insisted. "I traveled more than a moon upon my mare—straight south—to get here. I forgot your *paiza* and your message pouch at an arrow station, but I didn't steal them."

"Then how did you come to lay a hand upon the royal treasure in these bags?"

I saw my way out. Standing tall, I said, "One of your arrow riders slipped down a shale slope, breaking his arm and injuring his horse. I was told to ride in his place."

"And who told you this?"

"Why, one of your own soldiers," I answered proudly.

"And he did not give you a gold *paiza* and possibly a message pouch to deliver with it?"

I flushed. "Yes, great Khan. But . . . but a woman tried to steal my mare and I had to fight to get away from her and to deliver these important things to you. That's where I left the *paiza* and message pouch."

"A mare?" The Khan leaned forward. "My captain tells me you were riding a mare just now—a white one—that seriously lamed one of his best horses."

I nodded, my face burning. "I'm sorry. Is . . . is my mare . . . is she all right?" The stammered words sputtered to a whisper. Anxiously I twisted the middle fastening of my *del,* closing my eyes in fear as I awaited the Khan's answer.

In a regal voice rippling with indignation, Kublai Khan replaced my question with one of his own. "How dare you say 'my mare'? Were you not providing the services of an arrow rider?"

My eyes flew open; I sensed a new danger. Dumbly I nodded.

Kublai Khan's powdered face was twisting into anger. "Arrow riders serve the length and breadth of the empire, of which I am head; thus any horse galloping beneath them serves me. Which is to say, I own this white mare, not you."

"But . . . but . . ." I was stammering again, my mind grasping for an argument. "But I am not really an arrow rider, great Khan, for they are all boys."

As if slapped by my words, Kublai Khan roared, "Silence!" He narrowed his eyes and lowered his voice. "You have but to make a choice: if you were carrying these two bags away from Khanbaliq you are a thief and will forfeit your head; if you were carrying these bags toward Khanbaliq you are an arrow rider—girl or not— and everything you own belongs to me."

His last words screamed through my ears. I had heard them before and my cheek stung anew with the memory of the heavy-browed soldiers' leader spitting upon it. Again I saw the terrorized faces of my family and relatives as the soldiers charged into our *ail,* boldly stealing men and horses. I saw the two *urgas* choking Bayan and the rough hobbling of three legs. My fists clenched. The powder-faced man before me had authorized this mistreatment.

Shaking, I muttered between gritted teeth, "You're the thief."

"Again?"

"You're the thief!" I shouted so loudly that the leopard jumped up, switching its tail. Guards emerged from the shadows, lances raised. The Khan held up a hand and they halted.

"You stole my uncle and two cousins and all of our best horses. Your soldiers just rode in and—in your name— took what they wanted." I shook my fists. "You stole my white mare and I dressed as a soldier to stay with her. You can't have her because she's mine!" I stamped my foot and, to my dismay, nearly tumbled over.

Surprise replaced the Khan's anger. He regarded me anew. "You act more like the spur-footed cock than a crippled girl. Are you not afraid of me?"

"Should I be?" My reply was brazen, hiding, I hoped, the panic that weakened my knees.

The Khan pressed his lips together. "Yes . . . and no. I'm a fair man. When I am planning to capture a city I always extend an opportunity to surrender. That is more than fair. Should a city refuse my offer, I simply leave no living thing breathing." He shrugged his shoulders, nonchalantly raising his soft palms upward. "If your story proves true you will be treated just as fairly." A nod sent several guards hurrying from the room.

Turning, Kublai Khan tugged open one of the goatskin bags, snapping the wax seal. He dipped a hand inside and pulled forth a small leather pouch from which he drew out a silk-wrapped bundle. He carefully unwound the silk to reveal . . . a wedge of cheese. I'm sure my jaw must have dropped to my chest. I had risked my life, and the lives of my horse and cat, to deliver a bag of cheese? Then he was breaking open the other bag. Surely this one contained the gold and jewels. But after much untying and unwrapping his plump fingers plucked out a cluster of small dark balls—the oily fruit of the olive tree. He weighed each food upon an upturned palm, eyeing them as proudly as if they were riches. With evident pleasure he popped an olive into his mouth, bit into the cheese, and busily chewed.

"Now," he said after swallowing, "you have not enough years to be plagued with the gout. What has happened to your foot?"

The words rushed forth in a whisper. "The horse chose me."

The Khan stopped chewing. "What did you say?"

In a stronger voice I said, "I am told the horse chose me." Even at that moment I thought those were strange words to be speaking to a Khan and yet I babbled on.

"Chose you for what?"

"To sit upon its back and be one with it. To fly across the land and taste the wind upon my tongue. To feel my blood pounding with its hooves. And to listen to its words within my heart."

The Khan was staring into emptiness. And smiling. "To gallop down a hillside," he was saying, "to catch the *saiga* by surprise and—leap for leap—chase after him like the wind." He set down the cheese and braced his palms upon his wide thighs.

"You bring to me pleasant memories of my childhood upon the steppes. Of the great pleasure I took in riding." He sighed. "But many, many years have passed since I could throw a leg over the back of a horse."

With a grunting lunge, the Khan rose to his feet. He turned toward the large table, under which the leopard was stretched, eyes slitted in false sleep, and took a limping step. His weight swayed from side to side like a boat upon the water as he moved toward the intricately engraved bronze jars and urns that stood upon the table. The great Kublai Khan could no more walk a straight line than me!

The Khan poured himself a large swallow of a liquid that looked like *ayrag* and took a drink, then set down the gold goblet, and, leaning heavily against the table, spoke to me again.

"What I don't understand is your stubborn attachment to this one mare. What makes her worth your neck?"

"She's my friend. She'd risk the same for me."

Kublai Khan snorted. He shook his head. But a smile began playing about his lips.

"Did you know that I own ten thousand white mares?" he asked.

"So I have been told," I said, keeping up my guard.

"Would you like to see them?" The Khan spoke impulsively, as if the idea had just struck him.

My guard fell away. "Very much," I responded. My heart soared. This was where I was going to find my swift horse.

As though reading my thoughts, the Khan held up his hand. "Wait," he said. "You may yet be proven a thief and a liar, but at present you are one of my own people who has faithfully delivered these riches to me. For that I am grateful. What is it you most desire?"

"A swift horse." The words tumbled out of my mouth as if they had been waiting there a lifetime.

"A bold request," the Khan replied, although he smiled. "And why do you need a swift horse? Have the sheep in your herds sprouted wings?" He chuckled at his own joke.

But I was all seriousness. The time had come. "I need a swift horse so that I may win the long race at the festival—the one in Karakorum. I have to win the race so I can bring good luck to my family. It is very important."

"Yes, good luck is always important," the Khan said, equally serious. "That is why I have so many white mares, for they bring me good luck. And their milk"—he touched his lips with his fingers—"it is as sweet as the nectar from a flower. But come, I will show them to you now. And then we will see what we can do about your swift horse."

The biggest grin of my life settled upon my lips, spread-

ing so wide that I thought I would never stop smiling. As
we turned to leave, a small beautifully dressed woman
bustled into the room. The leopard only flicked its tail at
her entrance.

"Where are you going?" she demanded as she crossed
the room, blocking our path. "Hai-yun is on his way to
meet with you." She folded her arms and glared at the
Khan with authority.

"Not now, Chabi. We are going to check on the mares."

"The white mares again! Always you are more concerned with your beasts than with your soul!"

The Khan raised his hand in annoyance. "I do not wish
to discuss my soul and the gods with Hai-yun today. Tell
him I will see him tomorrow."

"You will see him today," the woman said firmly. "He
is here to present blessings for the journey to Shangtu.
And are we not leaving for there tomorrow?"

"I had hoped we could sneak away before he arrived."
The Khan giggled like a little boy and leaned forward to
kiss the woman called Chabi lightly upon the cheek.

The corner of her mouth lifted. "How long will you be
gone?"

"Not long, dear. We just want to see the mares and
then we will return."

"I will see that Hai-yun waits."

"Yes, dear one, see that he does." The Khan turned to
go and I with him, but Chabi stopped us.

"Who is this girl?" she demanded.

The Khan looked at me with surprise. "Why, I do not
even know her name. She has ridden a long journey to
bring me dried olives and my favorite cheese made by the
Merkid tribe near the shores of Lake Baikal." It was the
Khan's turn to demand now. "What do you call yourself?"

"Oyuna," I said. "Of the Kerait."

"Are you skilled with needle and thread?" Chabi asked, her arms folded in a masterful pose.

I nodded, for my early days had been filled with little else.

"Good," she said, nodding her head sharply. "When you return you shall help with the sewing. Half the palace seamstresses are sick in their beds. How we will be ready to travel to Shangtu tomorrow only the stars know!" Turning upon her heel, Chabi strode noiselessly out of the great hall.

The Khan looked at me with a boyish grin and cocked his head. "A bit of advice: I have found life to be easier when one does as Chabi desires. Now come."

26. To Test the World's Wisdom

$\mathcal{A}$s Kublai Khan and I returned from the ten thousand white mares—who drifted, grazing, across emerald green meadows like the pale down of the milk plant—he asked if I would like to look upon my mare.

"Yes!" I responded, nodding so enthusiastically that I must have set the curtains in our traveling box to jiggling. The Khan had told truth when he said he could no longer throw a leg over the back of a horse and so we moved toward the Imperial Stud inside a large gold and blue and red box set upon a cart and pulled by four black horses. Peeking through the curtains, I saw that everywhere people stopped their work to stare in awe at their ruler. I must admit my chest swelled with pride to be riding at his elbow.

When we reached the Imperial Stud, and even before I had climbed out of the high box, a young boy led Bayan by a knotted halter to us. Her coat had been brushed clean, the knots combed out of her mane and tail and her hooves shone with an oily gleam. Even to my eyes she had never looked better. Whooping with joy, I threw my arms around her and murmured greetings in her fuzzy ear. She nickered and nuzzled my shoulder playfully.

"So this is the white mare who carried you on your long journey," the Khan said, slowly limping a circle around Bayan. "She has seen more than a few winters, has she not?"

I nodded.

"And her off hind leg—it appears as if she favors it."

I nodded again, but no amount of criticism was going to dampen my delight in Bayan. To my mind that day she was more beautiful than any of the Khan's ten thousand mares—a delicate carving of jade come to mane-tossing life.

Kublai Khan continued limping around Bayan, studying her through the eyes of a horseman. "Still," he was saying, "she possesses a fine head, a large eye. The back is strong." He turned to me. "I will have this mare. And, as I am fair, what will you take for her?"

The words almost flew past my ears before I caught their meaning. What would I take for her? So stunned was I that my numbed mouth opened and closed several times before blurting a blunt response.

"Nothing," I said. Then, remembering to whom I spoke, "With all honor given to my Khan, I could not part with her."

"Come, come, child. You are young; this mare is old. You have no need for her. Yet one who has carried such pleasure to me must remain with me."

"I could not," I repeated, stepping close to Bayan's head and clutching the red halter possessively.

"I am Khan!" The words roared. I jumped aside. "I will not be denied!"

Immediate silence fell over the stable. I was painfully

aware of a hundred horse heads—ears pricked—swinging toward us, of stableboys halted in mid-step, of a great holding of breath.

A bravery again crept up my calves, stiffened my spine, and set my jaw. Holding my head high, I stepped close to Bayan's neck and, stroking it, looked directly into the Khan's reddened face.

"You own the power to take my mare from me," I said evenly. "But I will never sell her. Not to anyone."

"Then you will trade her," the Khan said, no longer shouting. The stable activity picked up as our voices lowered. Twirling an oxtail fly swatter, Kublai Khan spoke craftily, in the urgent words of a horse trader. "You tell me you want a swift horse, Oyuna." Drawing his arm through the air, the Khan said simply, "Choose one."

I felt as if the air had been knocked from my lungs. This conversation was taking place as in a dream, and it was exactly what I had been dreaming of. But one thing was wrong. In my dream I rode home with Bayan *and* a swift horse. Now the Khan was asking me to choose between them. I could not choose to give up my beloved white mare. I just could not.

"Bayan—" I began in a quiet voice.

"What?" the Khan interrupted, tipping his head toward me. "Speak louder."

"Bayan is . . ." I was struggling for words, for how could I explain our close connection? "My mother used to say that a good friend is like a walk in the moonlight. Bayan has been that kind of a friend for me. She understands me better than anyone ever has. And I her. For this reason she cannot be for sale, or for trade."

I waited for the Khan's tantrum. His dark eyes burned. But his next words were not angry.

"You gave a name to your horse?" he asked curiously. Blushing, I nodded.

"I have ten thousand white mares," the Khan said incredulously, "and not one of them carries a name."

"Bayan is . . . special," I murmured. My bravery had evaporated, leaving me awkwardly shy.

"What is it that makes this one old mare of yours so special? What has she done to earn the name of beauty and goodness?"

Already I had noticed that Kublai Khan possessed an eager mind, one seemingly open to new ideas, however strange. And so I told him the story of my journey, leaving out nothing—how I had found Bayan at the festival, how she had spoken to me. The great conqueror raised only one eyebrow then and asked if I could make my mare speak to him. He did not even appear angry when I said I didn't think so. I told him about Echenkorlo and how she had talked of the ten thousand white mares. I told him about the dangers we—Bayan, Bator, and I—had survived in lugging his heavy bags across mountain, through *gobi,* and to this oddest of lands where he had built his palace.

The Khan was a patient listener and he asked serious questions. He seemed especially interested in Echenkorlo and, holding up a hand at one point in my story, called a servant to his side and sent him running with orders to have a particular adviser meet him at the palace. By this time we were seated upon a brilliant blue *shirdik* unrolled in the shade of a large tree. Other servants carried silver trays of fruits and cheeses and porcelain vessels of mare's milk and set them around us. The young stableboy stayed within our sight, letting Bayan nibble upon sweet grasses.

When the servant had jogged away, Kublai Khan asked

me to go on. I finished my story quickly, ending with the importance of riding home with a swift horse so that I might win the festival race and carry luck to my family. The great ruler thought for a moment, then summoned another servant. As if he had not heard my last words, my most important ones, the Khan asked me to describe Bator, while the servant, it appeared, drew the cat's likeness upon a paper. Then the servant was ordered to prepare announcements, each requesting the safe return of the small tiger-striped animal, and to hang them at the city's outer walls. I looked at this world's most powerful man with warm gratitude and new respect.

When Kublai Khan and I returned to the palace's great hall, the air crackled with tongues from a hundred lands. I learned later that these were men of very great learning, called to Khanbaliq to share their wisdom with the Khan. Some of the men studied the stars, others the gods, and still others focused their minds upon illness and healing. Kublai Khan asked the men of medicine to examine my crippled leg and to say to him then how the horse had chosen me. Next he made me repeat to all of these wise men the story of my journey. Mostly they fastened their interest on Echenkorlo. In fact one of the shamans, a small dark-skinned man from a land you call Tibet, said he had known of Echenkorlo and that her powers had been much respected. He said she was a great seer into the future.

"Can you see?" this dark-skinned man asked me, stepping close and peering into my eyes.

I shook my head, but he and the others were not satisfied. They asked what Echenkorlo had taught me. I could name only a few herbs and their healing powers. Still their interest did not fade. The Khan handed them the leather pouch Echenkorlo had given me. Over loud exclamations they fingered the animal figures cut into its surface and carefully examined each of the items within. Digging inside, one wise man pulled forth the golden winged horse ornament. Holding it high, he looked at me accusingly.

"Where did you get this?"

"I found it," I answered in truth.

"Can you read the seared shoulder bones of the sheep?" another suddenly asked.

I winced. "Well . . . ," I began.

A firm "no" would have been better. For within moments the burned shoulder blades of a sheep, still holding the warmth of the fire, were set in my hands and I was commanded to predict the weather for tomorrow's journey to Shangtu.

I protested, but the shamans insisted and Kublai Khan, with a single solemn nod, made it known it was his wish as well. Sitting on the floor, I cradled the bones in my lap, turning them over and round until I found the journey lines. How I hoped I would find an answer that would satisfy all of these powerful men. I bent over them, studied with my eyes, and traced with my fingers. The lines ran deep and fairly straight; tomorrow's journey would be swift. I thought.

Raising my head, I said in as steady a voice as I could muster, "These bones say that the journey to Shangtu should be swift. I cannot foretell the weather, for I have not been trained in the ways of the shaman."

"You can hear animals talk," one black-robed man said.

"Only one animal," I protested. "And not always. And still I cannot make her speak to me."

A loud announcement from a servant interrupted our debate. Looking up, I realized that the entire afternoon had slipped past, for already the walls flickered with shadows from lanterns burning across the long walls.

The Khan lifted his hand and a shabbily dressed man

with a flat face, one of the earth-workers, I guessed, entered the hall. He was carrying a large woven sack that twitched with a life of its own. At the Khan's order, the man set down the sack and bent to loosen its neck. To his surprise, and the murmured surprise of the others, a small dark-colored animal leaped from the sack and sped in sheer fright across the floor. It veered behind the large table. Immediately a noisy snarling and hissing erupted. The leopard, stiff-legged, marched around the table. Its prey, hair on end and growling ferociously, backed steadily, though crouched for a fight.

I had instantly recognized the brave animal and called out, "Bator!" Without breaking the leopard's glare, my little cat continued backing, step by careful step, until he could turn and trot confidently to my lap. He crawled onto my crossed legs, tail switching angrily, and his green eyes glared at the roomful of people.

As chatter resumed, I heard the Khan chuckle and looked up to see him smiling appreciatively at Bator's bravery. Catching his eye, I smiled my thank-you.

That night I slept in the softest bed that I had ever lain upon. And with Bator curled beside me and Bayan safely cared for in the Khan's stable, I fell swiftly to sleep. So soft were the cushions beneath my body that I imagined I drifted on clouds. Yet not a dozen breaths after I closed my eyes, these clouds wrapped round my body and lifted me up—*swoosh!*—into the dark sky. Through the night we flew, silent as an owl's wings, across hill and *gobi* and mountain. All the way to the cave of Echenkorlo's grave! In the moldy blackness I was tossed from the clouds into the dirt, my chin landing sharply so that I stared at the drawings of a long-rooted flower and a stiffened horse and a gold *paiza* scratched into the mud by a dying hand.

27. My Life in the Palace

Every year Kublai Khan and his family and servants left the heat of summer in Khanbaliq to pass the months of June, July, and August at his palace in Shangtu. I never saw this northern city, but I was told it was smaller than Khanbaliq and that the Khan spent his days there hunting and feasting.

As the following day was the first of June, the palace shook with scurrying feet and shouted packing orders. Yet long after the sun rose, dripping heat from a hazy sky, the Khan's assembly was still waiting, swishing at flies, outside the city gates.

For this annual journey Kublai Khan traveled in a huge box lashed to the backs of four elephants. At this moment, however, he sat in the shade of a large tree and scowled. The great gray animals swayed with boredom, trunks scooping up dust only to toss it aside. The creaking of their harness was lost among the nervous bleating of goats, the cries of women hurrying their children, the restless whinnying of horses pawing the ground beneath empty saddles. At last Marco Polo, one of the Khan's advisers from a land an entire year's travel away, galloped up, full of news. He and Kublai Khan climbed into the box atop the elephants and the procession of a thousand feet began shuffling out of the city.

The Khan had asked me to stay behind and work the summer at his Imperial Stud. In our visit there the previous day he had noted that the horses readily responded to my touch, so, with the promise of a swift horse for a job well done, I began service as an assistant—gentling the yearlings and saddling the two-year-olds. Bayan needed a rest anyway, so I contentedly spent the warmest months in the company of my white mare and her new stablemates.

I found my service continuing, however, when Kublai Khan and his family returned to Khanbaliq in early September. Within the first few days of their homecoming Chabi sent a servant to summon me to the palace. All that summer, it seemed, she had remembered that my hands were skilled at sewing and now she spread garments before me and asked my thoughts.

Chabi, I knew, was only one of the Khan's wives, yet, like him, she carried an active mind that pounced upon new ideas. For this reason, and also because of the tenderness he showed in her presence, I came to believe that she was his favorite. On the day that Chabi called me into the palace sewing rooms she was designing a new style of *del* that had no sleeves. "So much easier for the archer to reach for his arrow, don't you agree?" she said. Oh, she was always trying new ways. Together we designed various styles of head coverings and we experimented with weaving rugs of everything from used bowstrings to dog hair.

When I wasn't with the horses, then, I was sitting beside the palace seamstresses, sharing stories and laughter. It was good in this strange land to speak with others in my own tongue. Now I sewed happiness into the garment upon my lap and wished that it might accompany its wearer like a sunbeam.

The Khan hadn't forgotten his promise to me. At times, in my travels between the stables and the sewing rooms, I would pass him. He always took a moment to greet me by name and, occasionally, to exchange a teasing word. Then the two limping souls in the palace, one young and one old, would lean against the walls and talk.

Always it was a joke with him that I had refused to sell him Bayan. "How is my mare?" he would ask, chuckling. "The one I call Bayan. Have you decided, Oyuna, which swift horse you will take for her?" And always I would answer that I was just trying out this chestnut or that bay, but I was not yet sure which one I would choose and perhaps I would decide tomorrow. But tomorrow was a long time coming.

More and more often the gold ornament that brought me luck was left inside Echenkorlo's leather pouch. I no longer needed to carry it with me at all times, I thought, for good luck seemed to have settled around my shoulders. I knew I had escaped the clutches of bad luck on many an occasion, most especially the night I slept beside the dead body of my grandmother, and I knew I would never do anything to tempt it to chase me again. Besides, I was happy now. I was even ready to return to my family. But my journey would have to wait a little longer. I had been watching my white mare with a close eye and by October I was certain: Bayan swelled with foal.

The young girl pressed a hand to each cheek, framing a mouth that hung open in a silent O. With unblinking eyes she watched first one small hoof and then another—wrapped in a glistening blue pouch—slide from the round-sided mare. In a rush came the fine muzzle, the sculpted head, two incredibly long legs, and, spilling on top of them, a small body and two more spidery legs.

The gnarled hands of the old woman expertly tore away the pouch from the foal's face. A thumb quickly wiped clean each sucking nostril.

Slowly then the woman arose and gingerly stepped to the corner, sinking again into its shadows and pulling the young girl to her side.

"A fine filly," she whispered.

Tipping her smiling face to her grandmother, the girl whispered back, "You said that earlier. How did you know?"

The gold flecks twinkled in the dove gray eyes. "I have seen many births," she said simply. A cloud rushed across, chasing away the sparkle. "And many deaths as well." Her bony chest heaved a sigh. "I shall finish my story."

28. Spring 1281

*C*habi died in the spring. The Khan sat for days just staring out the window.

And the weather! It turned cold—so cold!—with rain, it seemed, that would not end. The crops began to rot in the fields.

My eyes puffed red and it seemed that the water would not stop flowing from them either. In Chabi I had again found the love of a mother. Losing her flooded me with memories of losing my own mother. During these days I think I closed my eyes for only a few moments at a time. For while the daylight delivered tears, the darkness behind my lowered lids called forth terrifying apparitions.

How awful the dreams that tormented me! As soon as I let my eyelids droop, grinning white horses galloped from the dark hollows of my mind. They charged straight at me, teeth bared, only to slide to a halt, as if suddenly frozen through. I watched in helpless horror as their hooves grew long, sinking into the black earth. Somehow I could see the hooves beneath the ground, pushing deeper, stretching longer, always turning brown as they twisted into tangled roots. As soon as the roots hardened, the horses stiffened and fell over and died.

"Tengri!" I called out upon awakening, sobbing. "Why is everyone and everything dying?"

My one bud of comfort in those days was Bayan, for life was still growing inside her belly. I did not know, at that time, the stallion. One of Genma's, perhaps, or the wild yellow *gobi* stallion or maybe even one of Kublai Khan's royally bred studs. So blessed would be Bayan's foal if it was fathered by one of the Khan's own stallions! Sitting alone in my room at night, Bator purring at my side, I once more pulled the gold ornament from the leather pouch to study the girl carrying flowers upon her galloping horse. Taking a cloth in my hand, I would polish it, again and again, wishing very, very hard as I rubbed for a healthy foal and an easy delivery for Bayan.

But it seemed that Tengri had turned his back on Khanbaliq, for bad luck continued to rain down upon us. Now word arrived at the palace that the Khan's white mares were sick, that some, indeed, had already died from a mysterious illness. Kublai Khan summoned his advisers but did not travel from the palace.

I paled at the news, for Bayan grazed with these mares. And it had been two days since I had last checked on her when the news of the sickness arrived at the palace. Scolding myself as the laziest of mare keepers, I hurriedly saddled a horse borrowed from the stable and rode out to the valleys. Rain had ceased for the moment. Weak sunshine was fighting to poke through blue-black clouds lumbering across the sky.

When I first saw the splotches of white against the

emerald green *shirdik* covering hill and valley, I breathed a sigh of relief, for they drifted, as always, in casual rhythm. But as I rode closer I noticed that some of the splotches weren't drifting; in fact, some appeared stuck into the grass as if it were mud. At the near edge of one valley, the long-robed shamans gathered around a particularly sick mare, pinching her skin and waving their hands about her. One of the wise men held a red clay bowl of burning incense below the mare's nostrils, while another one pried open her lip. He held a short knife in his left hand and I looked away, knowing he was about to practice Genma's cleansing cure.

I was riding past the backs of these men, searching the hills for Bayan, when my ears caught words that made me gasp.

"Better to kill them all. Now!" one shaman was arguing in a booming voice.

"No," retorted another, "only a few have died. We must find a cure for their sickness, for the sake of the Khan."

"It is because of the Khan that these mares are dying!" The first shaman was shouting now. "Have your toes not turned moldy—like the crops—in all this rain? The gods are punishing the Khan because he has displeased them. He has not followed the daily purification rituals that we have prescribed. His Chabi has died because of it. The crops are dying, so soon we will all starve. And now the sacred white mares are dying. It is the gods' will that they die, I tell you. And if we kill the rest of them—now— perhaps the gods will chase away the rain and smile upon us as they used to do."

I saw that most of the shamans frowned at these heated words, although the man who spoke them stood nearly a head taller than them. "You cannot kill the Khan's mares without his permission," one of them warned.

"I will get his permission!" screamed the hot-tempered man and, robes swirling around his feet, he strode toward the city. A few paces from the group he threw his hands into the air and shouted to no one in particular, "They're all going to die anyway!"

I dug my heels into the horse I was riding, a pointy-crouped sorrel gelding, sending him plunging across the valley. My head turned from side to side like a banner in the wind as I searched for Bayan. Usually she grazed with one of the bands of older mares among the tall, juicy grasses at the river's edge and so I reined the gelding toward the swirling brown water. The mud sucked noisily at his hooves as they stomped through the yellow-bottomed rushes.

I had tied the jade pendant given to me by my mother around Bayan's neck so that I could more easily spot her among the white mares and also so that if her foal's birth began when I wasn't nearby, it would slip more easily from her belly. Ahead of us now, alarmed at our rapid approach, dozens of swanlike white necks popped up from the grasses. Around one of them I saw dangling the small pale green figure of a galloping horse.

Mid-stride, I slipped off the sorrel and pushed my way through the white bodies, all the while studying Bayan's face. Throughout the winter her eyes had glowed with an inner contentment. Today as I met her gaze I was certain I found no sickness, yet the luster seemed absent, the hollows above her eyes seemed deeper. I ran my hands over Bayan's brow, down her neck, and across her back. There was no fever, no stiffness. As usual, she reached around to nuzzle my shoulder with her playful lips. I breathed a sigh of relief, yet sat with her all that day while she grazed as we used to do upon the steppes of my homeland. And I promised to sit with her every day until she delivered her foal, which, by the swollen girth of her belly, could be at any time.

The following morning I huddled, waiting, against the trunk of a large shade tree, but the rain still blew and spit into my face. Not only the chill breeze sent shivers along my spine, but the horrid sight of more mares stretched painfully still upon the hillsides, only their wind-whipped manes aflutter. Tears brimmed in my eyes as I watched frantic foals nudge the unfeeling sides of their dead dams, then wheel, squealing, to gallop in circles. And I watched the shamans, like the unstoppable rise of murky flood-waters, march across the valley, shoving incense into each mare's nostrils, a knife into each mare's pale gum.

They didn't reach Bayan and the band of older mares until the third day. I protested loudly, but what is the voice of a girl against the gathered wisdom of many lands? I could only turn my head against the cruel stabbing and try to hold back my vomit. When the shamans marched on, I tugged on Bayan's forelock to lead her to the river. Scooping the muddy water into my hands, I managed at least to wash the dripped blood from her neck and chest.

The next morning when I rode out to sit with Bayan, she seemed to walk more stiffly than usual. My heart jumped into my throat. I tried to tell myself that these mornings were cold, that Bayan was just growing stiff with age. But all that day she shrank back when I pulled upon her forelock, trying to coax her into moving around to warm her limbs. By afternoon she was sick, just like the others, standing stiff-legged and miserable. Wringing my hands, I limped circles around her, begging her to tell me what was wrong, begging her to speak to me and let me know what I could do. Perhaps, I thought at last, even she didn't know.

On the day that followed, I was standing in front of Bayan, cupping her muzzle in the warmth of my hands, when I felt it press into them. Only the weight of a feather, yes, but it was movement! I searched her black eyes. The veil of pain that clouded them squeezed my heart. And then, through the pain, came that piercing look that went straight through me. Breathless, I waited for her to speak, but only a ringing emptiness filled my head. Tears filled my eyes.

Then, with an all-out effort, Bayan somehow managed to drag one sharp hoof across the muddy ground. The pale, bulbous ends of grasses, their fingery roots dangling like spider legs, lay upturned in the sunlight. Was she hungry? I wondered. Bayan had eaten the bulbs of plants when we crossed the *gobi*, but then only in order to survive. Here she had plenty to eat.

Bending to finger the exposed bulb and its roots, I remembered with a shudder the dreams I had been having about the stiff legs of horses turning into brown roots— the dreams I had been having ever since I passed the night in the mountain cave of Echenkorlo.

And then two more images crowded into my mind. The first was a memory that, among the bags of herbs and powders I had buried with my grandmother, were half a dozen large bags of brown roots. And second, that the drawing of the flower upon the cave's mud floor was not only of flower and stem but also of root—a long one. Perhaps, I reasoned, the root in that drawing was more important than the flower.

And, like beads upon a string, all the images fell into

order. The root, the stiff horse, the *paiza*—the plain message was that the roots in the bags were to be carried to
the Khan for his sick horses. Had Echenkorlo, I wondered,
foreseen the sickness that had befallen the Khan's horses?
Had she been carrying their remedy here?

Already I was turning from Bayan, climbing onto the
stable horse, and galloping toward the Khan. And still I
was thinking. About the dreams I had been having. The
grinning white horses in my dreams, I now realized, gri-
maced in pain, just like the stiff white mares. I shivered.
Had my dreams also foretold the mares' sickness? Did
that make me a shamaness? I shook that absurd idea from
my head and went on thinking as the stable horse went
on galloping.

Galloping! I thought with sudden alarm. Galloping just
like the girl in the gold ornament, carrying flowers in her
hand. Flowers with roots, I was willing to wager. Another
chill skipped up my spine. Had I, Oyuna, been chosen all
along to deliver the healing roots to the Khan, to save his
horses? The gold ornament had always brought me luck.
Perhaps it was meant to bring luck to the white mares—
and Bayan!—as well.

Luck. I reined the horse to a walk while I thought about
that troublesome matter. How was I to know I was right?
How was I to know if this was what the gods wanted? At
least one of Kublai Khan's wisest men seemed certain that
the gods wanted the horses to die. Who was I, a mere
girl, to say otherwise? All my life, I thought, I had been
ignoring the well-marked signs of bad luck and rushing
headlong into danger. Images charged through my mind:
a killing bolt of lightning, a sneering doll, a knife plucked
from the fire, Echenkorlo's bony hand stretching toward
me. I shook my head. Somehow I had lived. But my

mother was dead. Echenkorlo, too. How could I even think of pitting my own desires against the wishes of the gods? Oh, how was I to know what to do?

And then I found myself doing something that afternoon that widened not only my eyes, but the eyes of others. Riding directly to the shamans' smoky pavilions within the city's walls, knowing full well that they would all be with the Khan's mares, I asked one of their servants for freshly cleaned sheep shoulder blades. I boldly lied, saying that the Khan wished me to have them, and so, of course, I was handed a set from a large basket brimming with bloodstained bones.

Then I rode back outside the city gates and down to a secluded spot beside the river. I gathered wood and built a fire, and placed the shoulder blades within the flames. And then, limping, I paced the riverbank, back and forth and back and forth, thinking all the time: Should I travel this journey or not? Should I travel this journey or not? I watched the flames lap at the bones. Through their translucent lips I saw the heat-hardened cracks drawing me an answer.

At last the flames died down and, holding my breath, I dragged the bones from the fire with a stick. I pushed and poked the hot blades, turning them over several times until, in the fading light, I spotted the lines foretelling journeys. Squatting upon the ground, my heart pounding, I studied them. They started thick, traveled no more than a finger's width, and stopped. The answer was plain: there would be no journey.

Rocking back upon my heels, I blew a quick sigh of relief. Then I rose, kicked the warm bones with my foot, and sent them tumbling down the riverbank and into the river, where they sank from sight.

As if a great weight had been lifted from my shoulders, I galloped back toward the Khan's white mares. Perhaps Bayan was doing better. But the cold reality was that she was stuck to the same spot where I had left her. Dismounting and rushing to her side, I found her body cool to my touch. She couldn't paw the ground; she couldn't nuzzle me. I felt her drawing away from me, dying. I threw my arms around her hardened neck and sobbed.

Piercing my own noisemaking, the words silently etched themselves upon my brain: "Help us."

Looking into Bayan's eyes, I knew I had my true answer. Lurching wildly upon my twisted foot I ran back to the stable horse, climbed into the saddle once more, and galloped through the dusk to the palace. I knew that at this time of day Kublai Khan would be meeting with his advisers to plan the following month's ceremonies. No guard could stop me as I rushed through the palace and into the great hall.

"I know the cure for your mares," I called. Faces from all lands turned toward me in a mix of astonishment and scorn. Only Kublai Khan, with one hand raised to quiet the room, listened.

"What is the cure, Oyuna?" he asked as solemnly as if I were one of his respected advisers.

"W-well," I stammered, "I don't actually know what it is called, but I know where to find it."

The room's men jumped upon my hesitation. "How dare you claim a cure you cannot name?" one said. And, "What is your training that you can say this to the Khan?" But another muttered, "I told you she knows more than she is telling." Finally the Khan raised his hand again and immediately silence lay over the room.

"What makes you say this, child?" His voice was sad

but I saw in his eyes the spark of hope. I dared not fail him.

Taking a deep breath, I told Kublai Khan and his wise men about the drawings I had seen in Echenkorlo's cave. And I described to them the dreams that had tormented me almost every night since. I explained that the drawing in the cave of the stiff horse and the grinning horses of my dreams were, in this world, the Khan's white mares, stretched in sickness, their lips taut with agony. I added that, in my dreams, the horses' hooves turned into roots and that I had buried with Echenkorlo bag after bag of one kind of root which, I guessed, she must have been carrying to the palace. Echenkorlo was a seer, I reminded the shamans. She must have foreseen this sickness, for she left this message in the mud.

As soon as I finished, the room erupted in loud talk.

Above all the noise I heard the Khan ask, "Where is this cave?"

"Pay no mind to her—" one adviser began, but a mere glare from Kublai Khan pressed him into silence.

"How far is this cave?" he asked again.

"I'm not sure exactly . . . ," I said, which brought snorts and rolling eyes from the advisers. I spoke louder. "I do know the cave lies in the Hentei Mountains; it is near an *obo* and it is a day's ride south of one of your arrow stations, one managed by a woman—a rather large woman—named Genma."

"I know the station," volunteered a young soldier standing guard in the background. The Khan waved him forward. "I used to be an arrow rider along the northern routes," he continued. "I believe I could find the cave with the help of this girl."

The Khan looked at me, hard. He had to believe me,

for Bayan's sake. And so I stared, not even blinking, straight into his eyes. He spoke quickly. "Then find it," he commanded the soldier. "Take the girl here—Oyuna is her name—and ten men of your choosing—you as their leader—and fifty of my fastest horses—"

"Great Khan," interrupted one of the advisers. The ruler turned. "With all due honor to your decision, should we not consult the gods? To burn the shoulder blades will not take long."

My stomach knotted, for I knew what the bones would tell. "I have already—" I began to say, but it was my turn to be silenced by Kublai Khan. "Pack your things, both of you, while we decide this journey's fate."

The young soldier ran one way, I another.

Bator was sitting upon my bed when I reached my room, tail switching excitedly as if he already knew what was taking place. I whispered to him as I threw my few things into Echenkorlo's leather pouch.

"We're riding back to the cave, Bator. Tonight! We're going to try to save Bayan and all the others." I gave the cat a swift caress along his arching back. "If you can do anything, Bator, anything at all, please don't let her die."

When I returned to the great hall, several soldiers, all with large leather bags strung over their shoulders, began gathering. The shamans huddled over a brazier containing white bones.

The Khan looked up from his ornamented chair. "Unpack your things," he said sadly. "It would bring bad luck to ride forth upon this journey."

I shook my head vigorously, all the time feeling a prickle of fear upon the back of my neck. My voice, when I spoke, sounded loud to my ears. "I, too, read the blades, just this afternoon, and I know what they say. But I have also looked into the faces of the horses, and I have listened to them with my heart." A murmur traveled around the room. So I spoke louder. "I refuse the bad luck that is delivered." A gasp! "Instead I will make my own luck. And I will ride to the mountain cave and I will bring back the cure of the roots."

The Khan was shaking his head. "Well spoken, Oyuna. But I have had enough dying. There is no need for more."

"But there will be more," I pleaded. "All your horses will die if we don't ride to save them."

Kublai Khan stared across the multitude of wisdom-filled heads before him. I thought I saw a tear glisten in his eye, but this could have been my imagination, for I stood far from him. "The mares are my one remaining happiness," he said at last, looking at me. "Save them if you can."

A court official handed the young soldier a gold *paiza*. He gave me a glance and a nod, and we rushed into the night.

A hint of the coming dawn tinged the stable's mote-filled air. The spindly-legged white filly sucked noisily at her mother's swollen teats, stopping occasionally to stare, milk dribbling down her chin, at the two strange creatures whispering in the corner.

"And did you find the cave again?" the young girl asked eagerly.

"Yes," replied her grandmother. "We rode all day and all night, changing our horses at the arrow stations, and bandaging our sores with strips of cloth, then bandaging our bandages. In five days we passed

over the ground it had taken Bayan, Bator, and me
nearly a moon to cover. As if our travel was directed
by eyes in the heavens, our journey ran straight and
true. On the sixth day we climbed into the mountains
and right into the meadow with the *obo*. So exhausted
were we—dizzy even—yet so happy! Together we
bowed nine times and circled the *obo,* all the while
thanking the mountain spirit for leading us there. In a
few more panting breaths we were at the cave.

"All of the Khan's soldiers stood away from the
cave's mouth, muttering nervously among themselves, for they knew a dead body lay inside. All
of the soldiers, that is, except the young guard named
Adja, the one who had led us there. He marched
confidently at my side as I entered the cave's shadows
to point to Echenkorlo's drawings, now almost
obscured by animal tracks. Already I liked this young
man." The woman smiled shyly and squeezed
the girl's arm.

"We called to the other soldiers then and, working
side by side on our knees, tore away the rocks and
branches I had piled at the small back of the cave. And
at last before me again was my own grandmother.
The men hid their faces from the sight of the dead,
but to me she looked peaceful—the smile upon her
waxen face content. I pointed to the large bags
containing the brown roots and each soldier dragged
one outside.

"Left alone with my grandmother, I whispered to
her. 'I listened with my heart,' I said. 'And I pulled
my own luck from the air.' I felt my gold ornament,
the one I had slipped into my pocket the evening
we flew from Khanbaliq, shift weight. And for the first

time, it felt unnecessary. The soldiers were returning to help me rebuild the burial wall, but I knew my task was not yet finished. Mirroring Echenkorlo's contented smile, I lifted the gold ornament and tucked it into my grandmother's pocket. 'I no longer need this,' I said, patting her worn *del*. 'May its luck be yours.'

"With nimble hands we piled the stones back upon the grave, climbed into our saddles, and raced down the mountain."

When the woman paused, as if her story was finished, the young girl looked up. Breathless questions tumbled one over the other. "Did the roots work? Did you return in time to save the horses? Did you save Bayan?"

The old woman bit her lip, grateful that the still-dusky stable hid her glistening eyes. In a voice suddenly grown tired, she labored on.

29. Bayan's Gift

Almost without sleep we again rushed across *gobi*, hill, and valley like a great gust of wind. When, at an arrow station, Adja peered closely into what must have been my very pale face, he ordered me to stay behind and rest. But fiercely I clutched the saddle with both hands and refused to step down. So he knotted a rope around my waist, also tying my feet into the stirrups. We thundered on along the ancient caravan route, my head nodding beneath one burning sun after another. I knew not the day. I knew not even if I slept or if I lived this exhausting dream. As the horses' hooves clattered upon the arching stone bridge that Bayan, Bator, and I had timidly crossed almost a year ago, the Khan's sentries immediately directed us to him, waiting with his herd of white mares.

The sight before my glazed eyes was worse than any that had haunted my sleep. Stiff-legged white bodies, like the oversized toys of children, lay toppled all across the green hills. Teams of men and oxen dragged the carcasses through the grass to a long black ditch that was being filled as fast as it was being dug. It looked as if the skin of the earth itself gaped with an open wound and that the men worked to stuff it with pieces of white bandage. Looking around, I saw that less than half of the herd remained standing. I feared we had returned too late. My eyes searched the grasses for Bayan while the shamans crowded around us.

One by one, we dropped the sacks, thudding, to the ground. The shamans fell upon them, picking through their contents like crows. Cackling and cawing to each other in strange tongues, they turned the roots over and over in their hands. I could tell that the men recognized the root, for several of them immediately referred to it as *gan-cao,* or licorice. Kublai Khan stood among the robed men, leaning upon a servant and looking more tired than I had ever remembered seeing him. He spoke with his advisers, asking of the root's healing abilities. After the briefest of discussions, the Khan shouted an order to administer the cure quickly to those of his mares that yet lived.

Echenkorlo's brown roots were hastily pounded into a powder, then small amounts were mixed into wide wooden bowls holding moistened grain. Most of the mares nibbled at the mixture, but those that were too stiff to move had their lips pulled wide and handfuls of the medicinal blend pushed down their throats. A call had gone out and already people from the city were arriving to dump their own small pieces of licorice root into waiting baskets. A group of women knowledgeable about the area's plants offered to scour the the hills and valley for more *gan-cao* plants.

With treatment of the mares well under way, I stumbled through the crowd to the Khan's side. He flinched when he saw me, then abruptly looked away. For what seemed like a great while, he loudly directed the lifesaving efforts of the shamans. I was horribly afraid of the answer to my question. But I had to know. Tugging at the Khan's silken sleeve, interrupting him, I asked.

"Bayan?" I said. "Is she . . ."

The Khan turned his sad dark eyes upon me. "Oyuna, my dear," he began, and I knew. He placed his hand lightly upon my shoulder as it began to tremble. "We tried so hard," I heard him say. "And your mare tried, too, I think, for she clung to life long past the time we thought she would die."

I could hold back my pain no longer. Tears poured down my face and I crumpled to the ground in overwhelming misery. The long, backbreaking journey to the cave, the nightmarish return with the healing roots—none of this had been worth my effort, for Bayan was dead. All those days I was gone had been wasted. Days I should have spent at Bayan's side, I told myself.

"Oyuna, Oyuna." The great Kublai Khan was bending over my shoulder, speaking only to me. "I share your sorrow. To lose a life mate is almost to lose life itself." His voice choked upon his words. Then, clearing his throat with a string of coughs, the Khan brushed at his eyes and straightened. In a more regal tone he announced, "I have had your mare buried upon my lands. It is what I wished. And I hoped you would agree." He paused, waiting for me to acknowledge his generous action. I stopped sobbing long enough to look up into his face. "Would you like to visit the grave?" he asked.

I nodded and somehow managed to climb to my feet. Stumbling at the swaying side of Kublai Khan, I was steered by his hand upon my shoulder across one of the grassy meadows to a spot where the riverbank was lined with drooping, long-leaved trees. By the very shape of their sagging limbs, these trees seemed to be weeping for my lost mare, my lost friend. Pushing our way through the pale green fronds, we arrived at a large mound of freshly turned black earth. I stared at it through swollen eyes brimming anew with tears.

"I don't know why things happen the way they do," the Khan was saying, "but I do believe that they happen for a reason. People will say that this mare we buried here never spoke to you, that your long journey to our court was pure chance, a whim of your own making." The Khan limped toward the tree's gray trunk and leaned his weight against it. "But you heard her words, Oyuna, and you must always believe that. And I, who have also learned to listen with my heart, believe that you were sent to our court for a reason: to help my white mares. For this I thank you and Bayan and that little tiger-striped cat of yours—he has a name, too, does he not? Anyway, he has been a complete nuisance in your absence and we have had to lock him in your room." The thought of Bator's antics made the Khan chuckle. Then he looked into my face with a tenderness that touched me. "There has been much sorrow in my life of late," he said, "and now there is sorrow in yours." He sighed. "Sometimes I miss Chabi so much that I wish my own life to end so that I may be united with her in the afterworld. But just when I am thinking about death, Oyuna, something happens that reminds me that life is not all sadness. And this time this gift comes from your mare."

The Khan looked over his shoulder and nodded once.

Turning back to me, he said, "I have told you that Bayan seemed to linger in half-death long after her time in this world had passed. It seemed to us that she was waiting for something. I thought it was for you. And that may be partially true, but she was waiting for another reason. To give you this."

A rustling behind us, punctuated by a shrill whinny, made me look over my shoulder. Pushing through the fronds now was one of the stableboys. And prancing between his restraining arms was a long-legged filly the color of spring snow. I looked at the Khan in amazement.

He nodded, smiling. "It is Bayan's filly. We had to help her, and it took a long time, but we managed to pull the small creature from her just as the spirit left her body." He tipped his head and studied the lively orphan, who reared straight up between the boy's outspread arms. "I rather guess by the bold eye and the long legs that the father resides in my Imperial Stud. Rightfully, then, I may lay claim to her. But I give her to you, Oyuna. To thank you. It was a lucky day when you rode into Khanbaliq."

A bittersweet salve was thus kneaded into my raw sorrow as I moved toward the bony foal. Taking her into my arms, I felt her heart rapidly pounding against my chest. "A lucky day," the Khan had said. Perhaps. But with the help of Bayan I had learned to make my own luck.

Pink light of morning dusted the two white bodies. The larger one, the mare, stood with her head drooped lovingly over the smaller one, her filly, which slept in a heap at her feet. In the corner, the wrinkle-faced woman made a move to rise.

"Wait, Grandmother," the girl cried, placing a hand upon the heavily robed arm. "You are not finished."

Cocking her head, the old woman settled back.
"What more do you wish to know, child?"

The girl's hands fluttered impatiently in the air.
"Everything! Like . . . like . . . what happened to
the Khan's white mares?" she stammered. "Did they
live? And . . . and what did you do? Did you stay
in the palace? Did you go home? What about Bayan's
filly?"

The old face creased in a patient smile. "Most of
Kublai Khan's white mares that were still living
continued to do so. The powdered roots seemed to
chase away the sickness. As for me, well"—she
exhaled a long breath—"I was not born to live in the
city. My heart was crying for the steppes."

"Did Adja go with you?"

Grinning, the woman nodded. "Yes, as my husband.
And Bayan's filly went and—thanks to the Khan's
great generosity—ten of his sacred white mares, ones
of my own choosing. The shamans could not believe
their eyes when I rode from the gates of Khanbaliq
herding ten royal mares and the loveliest of white
fillies."

A look of sorrow touched the girl's face. "But . . .
you never got to ride the long race, did you? Oh,
that's sad."

With a knobby forefinger the old woman teasingly
thumped her granddaughter's head. "You think it
was not a long race to gallop from Khanbaliq all the
way to the Hentei Mountains, then back?" She
shook her head and chuckled. "Yes, I did get to race
at Karakorum, although it was four years later and
I was pregnant with your mother."

30. The Festival Race

$\mathcal{A}$dja and I did not have far to travel to Karakorum, since we were living with his people, the Naiman,
just west of the famous city. But every bouncing step of
that journey yet lies indented in my memory for, with
your mother growing in my belly, I was saddled with the
early sickness. Curled upon the folded felt in the cart bed,
I tried not to groan when each jolt splashed a new wave
of nausea across me. Adja held the reins to the ox, but it
was I who had to shout to urge the animal along, for my
husband, having stamped his boot uselessly against this
trip, sat stiff-jawed and silent.

When I had first suspected my condition, I kept it a
secret. The time was late summer and Bayan's filly, whom
I had named Baltozi, meaning "steady joy," was maturing
into peak form. While she possessed her mother's beauty,
the exquisite creature remained small and fine of bone;
thus I had had to be extra careful in toughening her legs.
What would have taken a year or a year and a half with

any other horse had taken twice that long with Baltozi. The pounding race posed a risk to her bones, a double risk to my pregnancy, but . . . well, I was having dreams again—dreams of Bayan, this time—and I knew we had to try. I promised myself I would tell Adja after the festival, but the sickness took hold and I could not keep the news from him.

Such arguing that followed! In the years since meeting and marrying at the Khan's palace, we had lived as if cut from the same cloth, never disagreeing. Now we traveled, third in a line of four carts from our *ail*, without speaking. So I hugged the warm body of my constant companion Bator—fatter now and inclined to long naps—to my queasy stomach and thought about our last journey to Karakorum.

It had been with my father. As then, I was approaching the festival with a mixture of hope and dread. This time my hope was pinned on winning the long race, yet I somewhat dreaded the idea of seeing my father and Shuraa again. Oh, I wanted to see them, to let them know that I was all right and very, very happy; but I worried that they would still be angry with me for riding off with the soldiers and not looking back. My fretting gnawed at my weakened stomach for three entire days before our ox came to a bellowing stop one noon outside Karakorum's walls.

Only after Adja and I had set up our *ger*, and—still with few words—brushed Baltozi and tended the animals and made a pieced-together meal of the wonderful festival foods, did I hesitantly ask my husband to help me find my father. To my surprise, Adja threw himself into the quest, hoping, I began to think, to steer my resolve away from the race. Dropping the last chunk of *aaruul* into Bator's waiting mouth, he immediately took my arm and we set out through the crowds, asking this person and then that one for the whereabouts of my *ail*. But there are many fish in the river and they don't come when you call. The best we could do that first evening was to tell any of the Kerait people that we met that I, Oyuna, would be riding a white mare in the long race and to please pass the news to my father.

Between my bouts of nausea, when I lay curled within our *ger,* Adja and I spent the next two days holding hands and letting ourselves be overwhelmed by the festival's riotously colorful sights and merry, though raucous, noises. The night before the long race, as I laid out the new *del* I had been saving for the event, my husband tried one more time to keep me from stepping into the saddle.

"Oyuna," he implored, pulling me to him, "please, you are the fire in my heart. How could I go on living without you? And feel," he said, placing his hand upon my still-flat stomach, though it brushed my breasts, which already swelled expectantly. "Our child blossoms inside you. Do not risk both your lives for a meaningless race."

"It's not meaningless," I argued for the hundredth time in the past moon.

"But the Khan himself—"

"I know, dear one," I said more gently, laying my palm upon the leathery check of my beloved Adja. "Kublai Khan himself said on our parting that the race I ran— that we both ran—to my grandmother's burial cave carried more luck to him than I could ever hope to find by winning the festival's long race. I understand that now. But the race tomorrow is no longer about winning luck. It's about closing the circle."

Adja wrapped his arms around me and chuckled softly. "Dreams again?"

I elbowed his ribs. "Don't you laugh at my dreams. We saved the Khan's white mares thanks to such dreams."

"I know, I know," he said, stroking my hair. "Tell me about the circle."

I pushed myself upright, staring intently into the cooking fire. "The last time I was in Karakorum is when I met Bayan. I was looking for a swift horse, for I had already set my mind on someday winning the long race. And I chose Bayan—or she chose me." I shook my head, for I had never been clear on who had done the deciding. "Of course, when I realized the weakness in her leg and the great many frosts that had passed over her back I knew she would never carry me in the long race. But you see"— I looked into Adja's eyes—"Bayan was planning even then for me to win that race. We just had some other things to do first. And now I am back in Karakorum, full circle, and I have Bayan's filly with me. And Baltozi is every bit the likeness of Bayan in her youth."

Adja looked skeptical. I hurried on. "In my dreams I have been seeing Bayan as she was when she was young—"

"How do you know it is Bayan?" Adja interrupted.

I placed my fingers upon his lips. "I just know," I answered. "I see Bayan—slender and white and strong— galloping across the steppes, leading all the other horses in a wild dash. And then I see her in a festival race—I am pretty sure it is Karakorum—and there is a boy upon her back and they are speeding beneath the banners at the finish line: they have won!" Transported to my dreams, I smiled. Then I caught the doubt in Adja's eyes. "I don't know when all these things happened," I said defensively. "But I know I am seeing Bayan and I know that I did find my racing champion at Karakorum. Bayan had to carry me on a long, slow journey when I thought I was plagued by bad luck. And then, before she died, she gave me her foal, that I could win the race we had set our hearts upon."

"And that's why we're here," Adja said.

"And that's why we're here," I repeated. "To finish what was started. To close the circle." Hugging my knees, I stared into the fire. An ember glowed hot, briefly taking the form of a galloping horse, neck stretched into the wind, before turning to white ash and falling away. I smiled once again. Confidence hardened within my bones and when I lay beside Adja that night I slept soundly.

Before dawn I was awake, the glowing green eyes of Bator blinking at me in the darkness. He knew the day, for he set aside his usual hungry wail to skitter madly around the *ger* once, ears pinned. A delirious yowl carried him past the door flap. The excitement stirred my sickness and I had to concentrate very hard on not vomiting while I slipped into the new silk *del* the deep dark red of a spring peony. A yawning Adja arose while I braided my hair into two short ropes. Without so much as a bowl of tea, then, we bolted from our *ger* to saddle Baltozi.

The young snow white mare saw us coming and raised her neck to nicker a greeting, tremulous with emotion. She knew, too. Nervousness overcame me and last night's confidence dropped away like so much ash. Coaxing the bit into Baltozi's mouth, I felt dizzy, tingly, and frightened in rapid turn. I began fumbling with the saddle fastenings. Adja placed his large hand over mine and I looked up into his smiling face, though I sensed he struggled to hide his concern.

"You'll do fine," he said in a husky voice. "Both of you."

"All three of us." I laughed, placing my hand upon my belly.

Adja's smile fled. "Please be careful," he murmured.

"I will," I promised. Adja moved to Baltozi's head, fussing with the headstall and smoothing strands of her long white mane. From the corner of my eye I saw him pull something out of his pocket and continue about his grooming.

Carefully I tucked away the end of the second girth strap and dropped the stirrup back into place. "What are you doing?" I asked. Adja didn't reply, only stepping aside and ducking his head sheepishly. Looking back, I saw that a lustrous silk tassel of sky blue dangled below Baltozi's throat. At its clasp, cast in gold, twirled the small figure of a horse, legs extended in a ground-covering gallop.

"I know, I know," Adja said. "You make your own luck. But I bought us a little extra anyway." Grinning, he leaned over and kissed me lightly on the cheek. "Ready?" he asked.

I fought back a strong wave of nausea and forced myself to match his grin. "Ready!" I answered. He cupped his hands at my knee and I stepped into them, easily swinging my leg over Baltozi's back. The familiar feel of the saddle—I had spent a thousand days in its wooden seat—immediately soothed my nerves. With Adja at the stirrup, we moved toward the starting line outside Karakorum's north wall.

In the coppery glow of dawn I saw scores of other horses and riders moving in the same direction, the animals neighing excitedly to one another, the riders, for the most part, sitting grim-faced and quiet upon the bouncy backs. A cool breeze skipped across the steppes, ruffling the horses' manes and fingering through their thick tails. Whimsically, it rose into a crisp blast, smacking the horses across their noses in a taunt. As if linked, the animals sucked the wind's challenge into their blood as one; its energy twitched through every hide. The powerful herd instinct grabbed hold and iron bits sawed uselessly to contain it. Shoulder to shoulder the horses began galloping, surging in a great wave toward the starting rope. Riders glanced uncertainly at one another, but something stronger than leather and iron and puny human arms had taken control. We gave in to the inevitable and bent over our mounts' necks as the mass gathered speed. I briefly noticed the starting man, mouth agape, drop the rope and scramble out of the way just as the first horses charged across the line.

I gave Baltozi her head, whooping loudly, and let the thrill wash over me as well. All the years of training and waiting and worrying and wondering were swept beneath Baltozi's pounding hooves. We were here! I whooped again. Then, shaking clear my head, I settled low into the saddle and set my sights on the knot of horses ahead.

We sprinted in a ragged group toward the first marker defining the long, looping course: a fluttering white banner anchored in a stack of rocks. But before circling it we had to get past a particularly tricky creek bed, with steep slopes of slippery shale. I watched as one horse and rider after another disappeared into the ravine, counted fewer climbing out of it. The deep creek bed scared me, but I had learned to trust Baltozi's instincts, as I had those of her mother, and when we thundered up to its lip, I hunkered down in the saddle, closed my eyes, and threw her the reins. I heard a loud grunt and a yelp as a horse and rider at our side painfully parted company upon the rocks. Pebbles kicked up by the fallen horse pelted my knee. But in a few heartbeats Baltozi was scrambling up the opposite bank and we were otherwise unharmed.

That first obstacle snatched its share of the racers.

Although some horses continued galloping riderless, the pack was easily cut by a few dozen. After rounding the banner, the course straightened toward a distant shallow pond, its rippled surface reflecting the golden light. A bold, sure-footed horse could save strides by carefully skirting the slimy shoreline and that's where I and some twenty other riders nosed our mounts. The jostling for position grew ugly as riders kicked and elbowed one another. A few horses were pushed into the water and ankle-deep muck and thus slowed. Another caught a hoof in the sucking ooze and took a skidding, nose-first fall, dumping his rider with a loud splat. I stayed just behind the main group, nimbly trying to steer a mud-spattered Baltozi through and around the pockmarked shore.

The middle of the course took us across a fairly flat area of the steppes, although one could never count out the possibility of stepping into a marmot hole and instantly snapping a leg. So certain was I that we were destined to run this race, though, that I didn't even squint at the ground ahead. I concentrated on pumping my hands against Baltozi's neck, urging her to greater speed; we began overtaking horses.

A lone, scrubby tree, sprouting almost at the feet of the remote mountains, served as our next marker. Baltozi and I galloped in the fifth position now, the majority of the pack strung out far behind. The racer immediately ahead of us was a rangy chestnut with a stride that ate up the ground. I watched his rump rising and falling for several leaps while I planned my strategy. Being so big, the horse, I guessed, couldn't make the turn around the tree very tight, so when he and his rider galloped in a wide arc, I nudged Baltozi to the inside and whipped around the tree so closely that I had to duck my head to avoid being pulled off by the branches. I heard the chestnut's rider shout angrily as we squirted past him, but Baltozi dug her heels into the sod and sped off.

A long gallop now until the next obstacle, yet another deep stream bed, so I settled Baltozi in behind the three leaders. She felt to be galloping easily beneath me. Of course, her neck was darkened with sweat and dirty lather bubbled around the saddle front, but I knew this meant she was in good condition. As the stream's cleft began to grow more distinct, I tightened my fingers on the right rein to steer Baltozi away from the others. You see, yesterday I had walked the course with my mare, studying where each hoof would fall. I knew where lay every treacherous stretch of sharp rocks, every mucky, grass-hidden bog. And I also knew that, off to the right, the stream bed's steep banks narrowed just enough that a horse might clear them in a single leap. It was a gamble, to be sure, but I was hoping that jumping the cleft, even away from the straightest path, would be faster than slowing down to scramble into and back out of the stream bed.

Blocking out vivid images of splintered bones, I headed Baltozi for the spot I had marked with three pale stones, urging her at every stride to hold steady and to make the effort. As if she read my mind, Baltozi pricked her ears at the stones and, at just the right moment, gathered herself, folded her front legs, and sprang into the air. For a heartbeat we were flying, my happiness in my mare soaring above us. The instant her front hooves hit, solid and ground-grabbing, I looked aside. The others were yet in the ravine's bottom. I tightened my fingers on the left rein and shouted to Baltozi. She pinned her ears and pounded faster.

As we pulled into line with the last marker, a small hillock with another white banner waving atop it, Baltozi and I were in the lead. I let a smile crease my face. Risking a peek over my shoulder, I saw that, while two horses threatened a few strides back, the third was tiring and rapidly falling behind. I lifted myself over the saddle's arching front to ease Baltozi's climb. She lunged upward, bunched her muscles, and lunged again. As lightly as a gazelle she bounded and, in the next instant, it seemed, we were atop the hillock and hurtling down the other side. Our appearance prompted a faint, far-off cheer. I looked up and, squinting into the morning sun, saw Karakorum again.

We had only one more stretch to gallop but this, more than any other part, was the real test of the long race. While the sun had been rising, the racers had been tiring. Only the grittiest horse, the one who could dig down and shove the air beneath heavy hooves, find another swallow of courage to keep driving, would win now. The race was no longer about speed; it was about heart. Bending over the white neck, I called past the labored breathing, "You can do it. It's your race."

And I swear to you that at that moment a mare's shrill whinny answered my call. It was sent from Bayan, for I would remember her voice forever. The tears that jumped from my eyes—I would later say they came from the wind whipping my cheeks, but the knot in my throat told otherwise. Half-blind then at the end, I crouched atop a speeding horse, clutching mane and flopping reins and hoping we would thread the crowd and cross the finish line without knocking someone flat.

We rushed toward the throng—or was it they toward us?—but all at once people surrounded us and I was trying to pull Baltozi to a stop, other hands reaching up to join mine on the reins. Suddenly limp, I more or less fell out of the saddle and threw my arms around Baltozi's sticky neck. Adja was at my side then, taking the reins from my hands and supporting my trembling body with his strong arms while smothering me with kisses. The men in the crowd hooted and the women clapped louder. Then a chuckle rippled through them as I tore away from my husband to throw my arms again around Baltozi's neck. Like her mother before her, she bent her sweat-beaded head to affectionately nuzzle my shoulder with her lips.

"Oyuna?" A man's voice made its way through the crowd's noise. "Oyuna, is it you?"

My father! I turned and stumbled into his outstretched arms, all of my questions and worries scattering in the wind.

Looking up, I saw such pride in his eyes that the lump climbed again to my throat, bringing with it fresh tears.

"This is my daughter!" he called happily to the crowd. "She has won!"

"That's the ending I wanted to hear." Smiling, the girl looked proudly upon the beautiful white foal who was just scrambling to her feet, testing wobbly legs. "Will my filly be swift?"

"She is the great-granddaughter of Baltozi, the great-great-granddaughter of Bayan. She should run, but I think there is more about her than speed."

"What do you mean?"

Ever so slightly, the old woman's head shook.

The girl spoke bluntly. "Grandmother, are you a shamaness?"

Dove gray eyes, flecked with gold, turned upon her. A gentle smile lit the papery face. "I look, and I

listen, granddaughter. Does not everyone?" Then,
cupping the girl's smooth chin in her calloused
hands, the old woman turned the round face up toward
her. One brown eye timidly stared back; the other
strayed weakly aside.

"I know others tease you because you are different.
And no one understands your pain more than I. But
you cannot let their words fasten the notion of bad luck
upon you."

Tears brimmed over the brown eyes. The chin
trembled.

"Do you understand why your mother asked me
here?"

The young head nodded. "I have to make my own
luck," came the whispered words.

"Yes, dear one." The gnarled hands released the
chin, pressed the head against a comforting
shoulder. Tenderly, the old woman stroked the black
hair of her granddaughter. "I will repeat to you what
my grandmother Echenkorlo told me. 'Listen with your
heart instead of your ears. And always, always,
follow your own path.' "

Suddenly the girl giggled. Ducking her head, she
turned to find the inquisitive filly tickling her ear
with long chin whiskers. Lightly she kissed the tiny
muzzle, then laid her cheek against the moss-soft
skin. The filly nudged her playfully.

A gasp jumped from the girl.

"What is it, granddaughter?" the old woman asked
calmly.

The girl looked in awe into the wisely nodding face
of her grandmother. "She—the filly, I mean—she
said she's ready."

GLOSSARY

aaruul   a hard, yellow cheese made from the milk of camels, cows, goats, or sheep

ail   a group of herdsmen and their families traveling and camping together

Almas   a legendary half-man, half-beast; the Abominable Snowman of Mongolia

arban   a military unit of ten soldiers

arslan   lion

ayrag   fermented mare's milk

boal   a drink made of honey

bustard   a large, sturdy-legged bird, similar to a turkey

del   a thick wraparound robe with a stiff, stand-up collar; the traditional Mongol garment

gan-cao   the Chinese name for the licorice plant; its powdered root can be eaten to counteract toxins in the body

gentian   a blue-flowered plant that can be used to reduce swelling

ger   a circular tent made of layers of felt stretched over a wicker frame *gobi*   an area of hard soil strewn with gravel and sparse vegetation

Golden Nail   the North Star

Itugen   goddess of the earth

khuruud   a hard, sun-dried curd

Koke Mongke Tengri   supreme deity of the Mongols; literally, the "Eternal Blue Sky"

kulan   a wild ass

lama   a member of the Buddhist religion practicing celibacy and living in a monastery

marmot   a large rodent living in underground burrows; similar to a woodchuck

mong   brave

morinkhour   a two-stringed violin-like instrument with a carved horse head in place of the scroll, played with a bow made of horsehair and wood

obo   a shrine

paiza   a passport; historically, a tablet made from such materials as wood, copper, or gold and carrying an inscription entitling the bearer to safe passage

saiga   a bulbous-nosed antelope

Sain bainu?   How do you do?

sandgrouse   a pigeon-like bird

Seven Giants   the Big Dipper

shirdik   the wool floor mat of a *ger*

suslik   a small, burrowing rodent similar to a ground squirrel

tarag   a thin yogurt

Tengri   *see* Koke Mongke Tengri

urga   a long pole with a leather loop at the end, used for capturing horses

usan   water